THE SECRET SHARER

ROBERT SILVERBERG

UNDERWOOD-MILLER
Los Angeles, California
Columbia, Pennsylvania
1988

THE SECRET SHARER

Signed edition: ISBN 0-88733-056-8
Trade edition: ISBN 0-88733-057-6

UNDERWOOD-MILLER
515 Chestnut Street
Columbia, Pennsylvania 17512

for Jozef Korzeniowski

THE SECRET SHARER

I T WAS MY FIRST TIME to heaven and I was no one at all, no one at all, and this was the voyage that was supposed to make me someone.

But though I was no one at all I dared to look upon the million worlds and I felt a great sorrow for them. There they were about me, humming along on their courses through the night, each of them believing it was actually going somewhere. And each one wrong, of course, for worlds go nowhere, except around and around and around, pathetic monkeys on a string, forever tethered in place. They seem to move, yes. But really they stand still. And I—I who stared at the worlds of heaven and was swept with compassion for them—I knew that though I seemed to be standing still, I was in fact moving. For I was aboard a ship of heaven, a ship of the Service, that was spanning the light-years at a speed so incomprehensibly great that it might as well have been no speed at all.

I was very young. My ship, then as now, was the *Sword of Orion*, on a journey out of Kansas Four bound for Cul-de-Sac and Strappado and Mangan's Bitch and several other worlds, via the usual spinarounds. It was my first voyage and I was in command. I thought for a long time that I would lose my soul on that voyage; but now I know that what was happening aboard that ship was not the losing of a soul but the gaining of one. And perhaps of more than one.

ROACHER THOUGHT I WAS SWEET. I could have killed him for that; but of course he was dead already.

You have to give up your life when you go to heaven. What you get in return is for me to know and you, if you care, to find out; but the inescapable thing is that you leave behind anything that ever linked you to life on shore, and you become something else. We say that you give up the body and you get your soul. Certainly you can keep your body too, if you want it. Most do. But it isn't any good to you any more, not in the ways that you think a body is good to you. I mean to tell you how it was for me on my first voyage aboard the *Sword of Orion*, so many years ago. I was the youngest officer on board, so naturally I was captain.

They put you in command right at the start, before you're anyone. That's the only test that means a damn: they throw you in the sea and if you can swim you don't drown, and if you can't you do. The drowned ones go back in the tank and they serve their own useful purposes, as push-cells or downloaders or mind-wipers or Johnny-scrub-and-scour or whatever. The ones that don't drown go on to other commands. No one is wasted. The Age of Waste has been over a long time.

On the third virtual day out from Kansas Four, Roacher told me that I was the sweetest captain he had ever served under. And he had served under plenty of them, for Roacher had gone up to heaven at least two hundred years before, maybe more.

"I can see it in your eyes, the sweetness. I can see it in the angle you hold your head."

He didn't mean it as a compliment.

"We can put you off ship at Ultima Thule," Roacher said. "Nobody will hold it against you. We'll put you in a bottle and send you down, and the Thuleys will catch you and decant you and you'll be able to find your way back to Kansas Four in twenty or fifty years. It might be the best thing."

Roacher is small and parched, with brown skin and eyes that shine with the purple luminescence of space. Some of the worlds he has seen were forgotten a thousand years ago.

"Go bottle yourself, Roacher," I told him.

"Ah, captain, captain! Don't take it the wrong way. Here, captain, give us a touch of the sweetness." He reached out a claw, trying to stroke me along the side of my face. "Give us a touch, captain, give us just a little touch!"

"I'll fry your soul and have it for breakfast, Roacher. There's sweetness for you. Go scuttle off, will you? Go jack yourself to the mast and drink hydrogen, Roacher. Go. Go."

"So sweet," he said. But he went. I had the power to hurt him. He knew I could do it, because I was captain. He also knew I wouldn't; but there was always the possibility he was wrong. The captain exists in that margin between certainty and possibility. A crewman tests the width of that margin at his own risk. Roacher knew that. He had been a captain once himself, after all.

There were seventeen of us to heaven that voyage, staffing a ten-kilo Megaspore-class ship with full annexes and extensions and all virtualities. We carried a bulging cargo of the things regarded in those days as vital in the distant colonies: pre-read vapor chips, artificial intelligences, climate nodes, matrix jacks, mediq machines, bone banks, soil converters, transit spheres, communication bubbles, skin-and-organ synthesizers, wildlife domestication plaques, gene replacement kits, a sealed consignment of obliteration sand and other proscribed weapons, and so on. We also had fifty billion dollars in the form of liquid currency pods, central-bank-to-central-bank transmission. In addition there was a passenger load of seven thousand colonists. Eight hundred of these were on the hoof and the others were stored in matrix form for body transplant on the worlds of destination. A standard load, in other words. The crew worked on commission, also as per standard, one percent of bill-of-lading value divided in customary lays. Mine was the 50th lay — that is, two percent of the net profits of the voyage — and that included a bonus for serving as captain; otherwise I would have had the 100th lay or something even longer. Roacher had the 10th lay and his jackmate Bulgar the 14th, although they weren't even officers. Which demonstrates the value of seniority in the Service. But seniority is the same thing as survival, after all, and why should survival not be rewarded? On my most recent voyage I drew the 19th lay. I will have better than that on my next.

YOU HAVE NEVER SEEN A STARSHIP. We keep only to heaven; when we are to worldward, shoreships come out to us for the downloading. The closest we ever go to planetskin is a million shiplengths. Any closer and we'd be shaken apart by that terrible strength which emanates from worlds.

We don't miss landcrawling, though. It's a plague to us. If I had to step to shore now, after having spent most of my lifetime in heaven, I would die of the drop-death within an hour. That is a monstrous way to die; but why would I ever go ashore? The likelihood of that still existed for me at the time I first sailed the *Sword of Orion*, you understand, but I have long since given it up. That is what I mean when I say that you give up your life when you go to heaven. But of course what also goes from you is any feeling that to be ashore has anything to do with being alive. If you could ride a starship, or even see one as we see them, you would understand. I don't blame you for being what you are.

Let me show you the *Sword of Orion*. Though you will never see it as we see it.

What would you see, if you left the ship as we sometimes do to do the starwalk in the Great Open?

The first thing you would see was the light of the ship. A starship gives off a tremendous insistent glow of light that splits heaven like the blast of a trumpet. That great light both precedes and follows. Ahead of the ship rides a luminescent cone of brightness bellowing in the void. In its wake the ship leaves a photonic track so intense that it could be gathered up and weighed. It is the stardrive that issues this light: a ship eats space, and light is its offthrow.

Within the light you would see a needle ten kilometers long. That is the ship. One end tapers to a sharp point and the other has the Eye, and it is several days' journey by foot from end to end through all the compartments that lie between. It is a world self-contained. The needle is a flattened one. You could walk about easily on the outer surface of the ship, the skin of the top deck, what we call Skin Deck. Or just as easily on Belly Deck, the one on the bottom side. We call one the top deck and the other the bottom, but when you are outside the ship these distinctions have no meaning. Between Skin and Belly lie Crew Deck, Passenger Deck, Cargo Deck, Drive Deck. Ordinarily no one goes from one deck to another. We stay where we belong. The engines are in the Eye. So are the captain's quarters.

That needle is the ship, but it is not the whole ship. What you will not be able to see are the annexes and extensions and virtualities. These accompany the ship,

8

enfolding it in a webwork of intricate outstructures. But they are of a subordinate level of reality and therefore they defy vision. A ship tunnels into the void, spreading far and wide to find room for all that it must carry. In these outlying zones are kept our supplies and provisions, our stores of fuel, and all cargo traveling at second-class rates. If the ship transports prisoners, they will ride in an annex. If the ship expects to encounter severe probability turbulence during the course of the voyage, it will arm itself with stabilizers, and those will be carried in the virtualities, ready to be brought into being if needed. These are the mysteries of our profession. Take them on faith, or ignore them, as you will: they are not meant for you to know.

A ship takes forty years to build. There are two hundred seventy-one of them in service now. New ones are constantly under construction. They are the only link binding the Mother Worlds and the eight hundred ninety-eight Colonies and the colonies of the Colonies. Four ships have been lost since the beginning of the Service. No one knows why. The loss of a starship is the worst disaster I can imagine. The last such event occurred sixty virtual years ago.

A starship never returns to the world from which it was launched. The galaxy is too large for that. It makes its voyage and it continues onward through heaven in an endless open circuit. That is the service of the Service. There would be no point in returning, since thousands of worldward years sweep by behind us as we make our voyages. We live outside of time. We must, for there is no other way. That is our burden and our privilege. That is the service of the Service.

O**N THE FIFTH VIRTUAL DAY** of the voyage I suddenly felt a tic, a nibble, a subtle indication that something had gone wrong. It was a very trifling thing, barely perceptible, like the scatter of eroded pebbles that tells you that the palaces and towers of a great ruined city lie buried beneath the mound on which you climb. Unless you are looking for such signals you will not see them. But I was primed for discovery that day. I was eager for it. A strange kind of joy came over me when I picked up that fleeting signal of wrongness.

I keyed the intelligence on duty and said, "What was that tremor on Passenger Deck?"

The intelligence arrived instantly in my mind, a sharp gray-green presence with a halo of tingling music.

"I am aware of no tremor, sir."

"There was a distinct tremor. There was a data-spurt just now."

"Indeed, sir? A data-spurt, sir?" The intelligence

sounded aghast, but in a condescending way. It was humoring me. "What action shall I take, sir?"

I was being invited to retreat.

The intelligence on duty was a 49 Henry Henry. The Henry series affects a sort of slippery innocence that I find disingenuous. Still, they are very capable intelligences. I wondered if I had misread the signal. Perhaps I was too eager for an event, any event, that would confirm my relationship with the ship.

There is never a sense of motion or activity aboard a starship: we float in silence on a tide of darkness, cloaked in our own dazzling light. Nothing moves, nothing seems to live in all the universe. Since we had left Kansas Four I had felt that great silence judging me. Was I really captain of this vessel? Good: then let me feel the weight of duty upon my shoulders.

We were past Ultima Thule by this time, and there could be no turning back. Borne on our cloak of light, we would roar through heaven for week after virtual week until we came to worldward at the first of our destinations, which was Cul-de-Sac in the Vainglory Archipelago, out by the Spook Cluster. Here in free space I must begin to master the ship, or it would master me.

"Sir?" the intelligence said.

"Run a data uptake," I ordered. "All Passenger Deck input for the past half hour. There was movement. There was a spurt."

I knew I might be wrong. Still, to err on the side of caution may be naive, but it isn't a sin. And I knew that at this stage in the voyage nothing I could say or do would make me seem other than naive to the crew of the *Sword of Orion*. What did I have to lose by ordering a recheck, then? I was hungry for surprises. Any irregularity that 49 Henry Henry turned up would be to my advantage; the absence of one would make nothing worse for me.

"Begging your pardon, sir," 49 Henry Henry reported after a moment, "but there was no tremor, sir."

"Maybe I overstated it, then. Calling it a tremor. Maybe it was just an anomaly. What do you say, 49 Henry Henry?" I wondered if I was humiliating myself, negotiating like this with an intelligence. "There was something. I'm sure of that. An unmistakable irregular burst in the data-flow. An anomaly, yes. What do you say, 49 Henry Henry?"

"Yes, sir."

"Yes what?"

"The record does show an irregularity, sir. Your observation was quite acute, sir."

"Go on."

"No cause for alarm, sir. A minor metabolic movement, nothing more. Like turning over in your sleep." You bastard, what do you know about sleep? "Extremely unusual, sir, that you should be able to observe anything so small. I commend you, sir. The passengers are all well, sir."

"Very good," I said. "Enter this exchange in the log, 49 Henry Henry."

"Already entered, sir," the intelligence said. "Permission to decouple, sir?"

"Yes, you can decouple," I told it.

The shimmer of music that signalled its presence grew tinny and was gone. I could imagine it smirking as it went about its ghostly flitting rounds deep in the neural conduits of the ship. Scornful software, glowing with contempt for its putative master. The poor captain, it was thinking. The poor hopeless silly boy of a captain. A passenger sneezes and he's ready to seal all bulkheads.

Well, let it smirk, I thought. I have acted appropriately and the record will show it.

I knew that all this was part of my testing.

You may think that to be captain of such a ship as the *Sword of Orion* in your first voyage to heaven is an awesome responsibility and an inconceivable burden. So it is, but not for the reason you think.

In truth the captain's duties are the least significant of anyone's aboard the ship. The others have well-defined tasks that are essential to the smooth running of the voyage, although the ship could, if the need arose, generate virtual replacements for any and every crew member and function adequately on its own. The captain's task, though, is fundamentally abstract. His role is to witness the voyage, to embody it in his own consciousness, to give it coherence, continuity, by reducing it to a pattern of decisions and responses. In that sense the captain is simply so much software: he is the coding through which the voyage is expressed as a series of linear functions. If he fails to perform that duty adequately, others will quietly see to it that the voyage proceeds as it should. What is destroyed, in the course of a voyage that is inadequately captained, is the captain himself, not the voyage. My pre-flight training made that absolutely clear. The voyage can survive the most feeble of captains. As I have said, four starships have been lost since the Service began, and no one knows why. But there is no reason to think that any of those catastrophes were caused by failings of the captain. How could they have been? The captain is only the vehicle through which others act. It is not the captain who makes the voyage, but the voyage which makes the captain.

RESTLESS, TROUBLED, I wandered the eye of the ship. Despite 49 Henry Henry's suave mockery I was still convinced there was trouble on board, or about to be.

Just as I reached Outerscreen Level I felt something strange touch me a second time. It was different this time, and deeply disturbing.

The Eye, as it makes the complete descent from Skin Deck to Belly Deck, is lined with screens that provide displays, actual or virtual, of all aspects of the ship both internal and external. I came up to the great black bevel-edged screen that provided our simulated view of the external realspace environment and was staring at the dwindling wheel of the Ultima Thule relay point when the new anomaly occurred. The other had been the merest of subliminal signals, a nip, a tickle. This was more like an attempted intrusion. Invisible fingers seemed to brush lightly over my brain, probing, seeking entrance. The fingers withdrew; a moment later there was a sudden stabbing pain in my left temple.

I stiffened. "Who's there?"

"Help me," a silent voice said.

I had heard wild tales of passenger matrixes breaking free of their storage circuits and drifting through the ship like ghosts, looking for an unguarded body that they might infiltrate. The sources were unreliable, old scoundrels like Roacher or Bulgar. I dismissed such stories as fables, the way I dismissed what I had heard of the vast tentacular krakens that were said to swim the seas of space, or the beckoning mermaids with shining breasts who danced along the force-lines at spinaround points. But I had felt this. The probing fingers, the sudden sharp pain. And the sense of someone frightened, frightened but strong, stronger than I, hovering close at hand.

"What are you?"

There was no reply. Whatever it was, if it had been anything at all, had slipped back into hiding after that one furtive thrust.

But was it really gone?

"You're still here somewhere," I said. "I know that you are."

Silence. Stillness.

"You asked for help. Why did you disappear so fast?"

No response. I felt anger rising.

"Whoever you are. Whatever. Speak up."

Nothing. Silence. Had I imagined it? The probing, the voiceless voice?

No. No. I was certain that there was something invisible and unreal hovering about me. And I found it infuriating, not to be able to regain contact with it. To be toyed with this way, to be mocked like this.

16

This is my ship, I thought. I want no ghosts aboard my ship.

"You can be detected," I said. "You can be contained. You can be eradicated."

As I stood there blustering in my frustration, it seemed to me that I felt that touch against my mind again, a lighter one this time, wistful, regretful. Perhaps I invented it. Perhaps I have supplied it retroactively.

But it lasted only a part of an instant, if it happened at all, and then I was unquestionably alone again. The solitude was real and total and unmistakable. I stood gripping the rail of the screen, leaning forward into the brilliant blackness and swaying dizzily as if I were being pulled forward through the wall of the ship into space.

"Captain?"

The voice of 49 Henry Henry, tumbling out of the air behind me.

"Did you feel something that time?" I asked.

The intelligence ignored my question. "Captain, there's trouble on Passenger Deck. Hands-on alarm: will you come?"

"Set up a transit track for me," I said. "I'm on my way."

Lights began to glow in mid-air, yellow, blue, green. The interior of the ship is a vast opaque maze and moving about within it is difficult without an intelligence to guide you. 49 Henry Henry constructed an efficient route for me down the curve of the Eye and into the main body of the ship, and thence around the rim of the leeward wall to the elevator down to Passenger Deck. I

17

rode an air-cushion tracker keyed to the lights. The journey took no more than fifteen minutes. Unaided I might have needed a week.

Passenger Deck is an echoing nest of coffins, hundreds of them, sometimes even thousands, arranged in rows three abreast. Here our live cargo sleeps until we arrive and decant the stored sleepers into wakefulness. Machinery sighs and murmurs all around them, coddling them in their suspension. Beyond, far off in the dim distance, is the place for passengers of a different sort — a spiderwebbing of sensory cables that holds our thousands of disembodied matrixes. Those are the colonists who have left their bodies behind when going into space. It is a dark and forbidding place, dimly lit by swirling velvet comets that circle overhead emitting sparks of red and green.

The trouble was in the suspension area. Five crewmen were there already, the oldest hands on board: Katkat, Dismas, Rio de Rio, Gavotte, Roacher. Seeing them all together, I knew this must be some major event. We move on distant orbits within the immensity of the ship: to see as many as three members of the crew in the same virtual month is extraordinary. Now here were five. I felt an oppressive sense of community among them. Each of these five had sailed the seas of heaven more years than I had been alive. For at least a dozen voyages now they had been together as a team. I was the stranger in their midst, unknown, untried, lightly regarded, insignificant. Already Roacher had indicted me for my sweetness, by which he meant, I knew, a basic incapacity to act decisively. I thought he was wrong. But perhaps he knew me better than I knew myself.

They stepped back, opening a path between them. Gavotte, a great hulking thick-shouldered man with a surprisingly delicate and precise way of conducting himself, gestured with open hands: Here, captain, see? See?

What I saw were coils of greenish smoke coming up from a passenger housing, and the glass door of the housing half open, cracked from top to bottom, frosted by temperature differentials. I could hear a sullen dripping sound. Blue fluid fell in thick steady gouts from a shattered support line. Within the housing itself was the pale naked figure of a man, eyes wide open, mouth agape as if in a silent scream. His left arm was raised, his fist was clenched. He looked like an anguished statue.

They had body-salvage equipment standing by. The hapless passenger would be disassembled and all usable parts stored as soon as I gave the word.

"Is he irretrievable?" I asked.

"Take a look," Katkat said, pointing to the housing readout. All the curves pointed down. "We have nineteen percent degradation already, and rising. Do we disassemble?"

"Go ahead," I said. "Approved."

The lasers glinted and flailed. Body parts came into view, shining, moist. The coiling metallic arms of the body-salvage equipment rose and fell, lifting organs that were not yet beyond repair and putting them into storage. As the machine labored the men worked around it, shutting down the broken housing, tying off the disrupted feeders and refrigerator cables.

19

I asked Dismas what had happened. He was the mind-wiper for this sector, responsible for maintenance on the suspended passengers. His face was open and easy, but the deceptive cheeriness about his mouth and cheeks was mysteriously negated by his bleak, shadowy eyes. He told me that he had been working much farther down the deck, performing routine service on the Strappado-bound people, when he felt a sudden small disturbance, a quick tickle of wrongness.

"So did I," I said. "How long ago was that?"

"Half an hour, maybe. I didn't make a special note of it. I thought it was something in my gut, captain. You felt it too, you say?"

I nodded. "Just a tickle. It's in the record." I heard the distant music of 49 Henry Henry. Perhaps the intelligence was trying to apologize for doubting me. "What happened next?" I asked.

"Went back to work. Five, ten minutes, maybe. Felt another jolt, a stronger one." He touched his forehead, right at the temple, showing me where. "Detectors went off, broken glass. Came running, found this Cul-de-Sac passenger here undergoing convulsions. Rising from his bindings, thrashing around. Pulled himself loose from everything, went smack against the housing window. Broke it. It's a very fast death."

"Matrix intrusion," Roacher said.

The skin of my scalp tightened. I turned to him.

"Tell me about that."

He shrugged. "Once in a long while someone in the storage circuits gets to feeling footloose, and finds a way out and goes roaming the ship. Looking for a body to jack into, that's what they're doing. Jack into me, jack into Katkat, even jack into you, captain. Anybody handy, just so they can feel flesh around them again. Jacked into this one here and something went wrong."

The probing fingers, yes. The silent voice. *Help me.*

"I never heard of anyone jacking into a passenger in suspension," Dismas said.

"No reason why not," said Roacher.

"What's the good? Still stuck in a housing, you are. Frozen down, that's no better than staying matrix."

"Five to two it was matrix intrusion," Roacher said, glaring.

"Done," Dismas said. Gavotte laughed and came in on the bet. So too did sinuous little Katkat, taking the other side. Rio de Rio, who had not spoken a word to anyone in his last six voyages, snorted and gestured obscenely at both factions.

I felt like an idle spectator. To regain some illusion of command I said, "If there's a matrix loose, it'll show up on ship inventory. Dismas, check with the intelligence on duty and report to me. Katkat, Gavotte, finish cleaning up this mess and seal everything off. Then I want your reports in the log and a copy to me. I'll be in my quarters. There'll be further instructions later. The missing matrix, if that's what we have on our hands, will be identified, located, and recaptured."

Roacher grinned at me. I thought he was going to lead a round of cheers.

I turned and mounted my tracker, and rode it following the lights, yellow, blue, green, back up through the maze of decks and out to the Eye.

As I entered my cabin something touched my mind and a silent voice said, "Please help me."

CAREFULLY I SHUT THE DOOR behind me, locked it, loaded the privacy screens. The captain's cabin aboard a Megaspore starship of the Service is a world in itself, serene, private, immense. In mine, spiral galaxies whirled and sparkled on the walls. I had a stream, a lake, a silver waterfall beyond it. The air was soft and glistening. At a touch of my hand I could have light, music, scent, color, from any one of a thousand hidden orifices. Or I could turn the walls translucent and let the luminous splendor of starspace come flooding through.

Only when I was fully settled in, protected and insulated and comfortable, did I say, "All right. What are you?"

"You promise you won't report me to the captain?"

"I don't promise anything."

"You will help me, though?" The voice seemed at once frightened and insistent, urgent and vulnerable.

"How can I say? You give me nothing to work with."

"I'll tell you everything. But first you have to promise not to call the captain."

I debated with myself for a moment and opted for directness.

"I am the captain," I said.

"No!"

"Can you see this room? What do you think it is? Crew quarters? The scullery?"

I felt turbulent waves of fear coming from my invisible companion. And then nothing. Was it gone? Then I had made a mistake in being so forthright. This phantom had to be confined, sealed away, perhaps destroyed, before it could do more damage. I should have been more devious. And also I knew that I would regret it in another way if it had slipped away: I was taking a certain pleasure in being able to speak with someone — something — that was neither a member of my crew nor an omnipotent, contemptuous artificial intelligence.

"Are you still here?" I asked after a while.

Silence.

Gone, I thought. Sweeping through the *Sword of Orion* like a gale of wind. Probably down at the far end of the ship by this time.

Then, as if there had been no break in the conversation: "I just can't believe it. Of all the places I could have gone, I had to walk right into the captain's cabin."

"So it seems."

"And you're actually the captain?"

"Yes. Actually."

Another pause.

"You seem so young," it said. "For a captain."

24

"Be careful," I told it.

"I didn't mean anything by that, captain." With a touch of bravado, even defiance, mingling with uncertainty and anxiety. "Captain *sir.*"

Looking toward the ceiling, where shining resonator nodes shimmered all up and down the spectrum as slave-light leaped from junction to junction along the illuminator strands, I searched for a glimpse of it, some minute electromagnetic clue. But there was nothing.

I imagined a web of impalpable force, a dancing will-o'-the-wisp, flitting erratically about the room, now perching on my shoulder, now clinging to some fixture, now extending itself to fill every open space: an airy thing, a sprite, playful and capricious. Curiously, not only was I unafraid but I found myself strongly drawn to it. There was something strangely appealing about this quick vibrating spirit, so bright with contradictions. And yet it had caused the death of one of my passengers.

"Well?" I said. "You're safe here. But when are you going to tell me what you are?"

"Isn't that obvious? I'm a matrix."

"Go on."

"A free matrix, a matrix on the loose. A matrix who's in big trouble. I think I've hurt someone. Maybe killed him."

"One of the passengers?" I said.

"So you know?"

"There's a dead passenger, yes. We're not sure what happened."

"It wasn't my fault. It was an accident."

"That may be," I said. "Tell me about it. Tell me everything."

"Can I trust you?"

"More than anyone else on this ship."

"But you're the captain."

"That's why," I said.

HER NAME WAS LEELEAINE, but she wanted me to call her Vox. That means "voice," she said, in one of the ancient languages of Earth. She was seventeen years old, from Jaana Head, which is an island off the coast of West Palabar on Kansas Four. Her father was a glass-farmer, her mother operated a gravity hole, and she had five brothers and three sisters, all of them much older than she was.

"Do you know what that's like, captain? Being the youngest of nine? And both your parents working all the time, and your cross-parents just as busy? Can you imagine? And growing up on Kansas Four, where it's a thousand kilometers between cities, and you aren't even in a city, you're on an *island*?"

"I know something of what that's like," I said.

"Are you from Kansas Four too?"

"No," I said. "Not from Kansas Four. But a place much like it, I think."

She spoke of a troubled, unruly childhood, full of

loneliness and anger. Kansas Four, I have heard, is a beautiful world, if you are inclined to find beauty in worlds: a wild and splendid place, where the sky is scarlet and the bare basalt mountains rise in the east like a magnificent black wall. But to hear Vox speak of it, it was squalid, grim, bleak. For her it was a loveless place where she led a loveless life. And yet she told me of pale violet seas aglow with brilliant yellow fish, and trees that erupted with a shower of dazzling crimson fronds when they were in bloom, and warm rains that sang in the air like harps. I was not then so long in heaven that I had forgotten the beauty of seas or trees or rains, which by now are nothing but hollow words to me. Yet Vox had found her life on Kansas Four so hateful that she had been willing to abandon not only her native world but her body itself. That was a point of kinship between us: I too had given up my world and my former life, if not my actual flesh. But I had chosen heaven, and the Service. Vox had volunteered to exchange one landcrawling servitude for another.

"The day came," she said, "when I knew I couldn't stand it any more. I was so miserable, so empty: I thought about having to live this way for another two hundred years or even more, and I wanted to pick up the hills and throw them at each other. Or get into my mother's plummeter and take it straight to the bottom of the sea. I made a list of ways I could kill myself. But I knew I couldn't do it, not this way or that way or any way. I wanted to live. But I didn't want to live like *that*."

On that same day, she said, the soul-call from Cul-de-Sac reached Kansas Four. A thousand vacant bodies were available there and they wanted soul-matrixes to fill them. Without a moment's hesitation Vox put her name on the list.

There is a constant migration of souls between the worlds. On each of my voyages I have carried thousands of them, setting forth hopefully toward new bodies on strange planets.

Every world has a stock of bodies awaiting replacement souls. Most were the victims of sudden violence. Life is risky on shore, and death lurks everywhere. Salvaging and repairing a body is no troublesome matter, but once a soul has fled it can never be recovered. So the empty bodies of those who drown and those who are stung by lethal insects and those who are thrown from vehicles and those who are struck by falling branches as they work are collected and examined. If they are beyond repair they are disassembled and their usable parts set aside to be installed in others. But if the bodies can be made whole again, they are, and they are placed in holding chambers until new souls become available for them.

And then there are those who vacate their bodies voluntarily, perhaps because they are weary of them, or weary of their worlds, and wish to move along. They are the ones who sign up to fill the waiting bodies on far worlds, while others come behind them to fill the bodies they have abandoned. The least costly way to travel between the worlds is to surrender your body and go in matrix form, thus exchanging a discouraging life for an unfamiliar one. That was what Vox had done. In pain and despair she had agreed to allow the essence of herself, everything she had ever seen or felt or thought or dreamed, to be converted into a lattice of electrical impulses that the *Sword of Orion* would carry on its voyage from Kansas Four to Cul-de-Sac. A new body lay reserved for her there. Her own discarded body would remain in suspension on Kansas Four. Some day it might become the home of some wandering soul from another world; or, if there were no bids for it, it might eventually be disassembled by the body-salvagers, and its parts put to some worthy use. Vox would never know; Vox would never care.

"I can understand trading an unhappy life for a chance at a happy one," I said. "But why break loose on ship? What purpose could that serve? Why not wait until you got to Cul-de-Sac?"

"Because it was torture," she said.

"Torture? What was?"

"Living as a matrix." She laughed bitterly. "Living? It's worse than death could ever be!"

"Tell me."

"You've never done matrix, have you?"

"No," I said. "I chose another way to escape."

"Then you don't know. You can't know. You've got a ship full of matrixes in storage circuits but you don't understand a thing about them. Imagine that the back of your neck itches, captain. But you have no arms to scratch with. Your thigh starts to itch. Your chest. You lie there itching everywhere. And you can't scratch. Do you understand me?"

"How can a matrix feel an itch? A matrix is simply a pattern of electrical —"

"Oh, you're impossible! You're *stupid*! I'm not talking about actual literal itching. I'm giving you a suppose, a for-instance. Because you'd never be able to understand the real situation. Look: you're in the storage circuit. All you are is electricity. That's all a mind really is, anyway: electricity. But you used to have a body. The body had sensation. The body had feelings. You remember them. You're a prisoner. A prisoner remembers all sorts of things that used to be taken for granted. You'd give any-thing to feel the wind in your hair again, or the taste of cool milk, or the scent of flowers. Or even the pain of a cut finger. The saltiness of your blood when you lick the cut. Anything. I hated my body, don't you see? I couldn't wait to be rid of it. But once it was gone I missed the feelings it had. I missed the sense of flesh pulling at me, holding me to the ground, flesh full of nerves, flesh that could feel pleasure. Or pain."

"I understand," I said, and I think that I truly did. "But the voyage to Cul-de-Sac is short. A few virtual weeks and you'd be there, and out of storage and into your new body, and —"

"Weeks? Think of that itch on the back of your neck, Captain. The itch that you can't scratch. How long do you think you could stand it, lying there feeling that itch? Five minutes? An hour? *Weeks?*"

It seemed to me that an itch left unscratched would die of its own, perhaps in minutes. But that was only how it seemed to me. I was not Vox; I had not been a matrix in a storage circuit.

I said, "So you let yourself out? How?"

"It wasn't that hard to figure. I had nothing else to do

but think about it. You align yourself with the polarity of the circuit. That's a matrix too, an electrical pattern holding you in crosswise bands. You change the alignment. It's like being tied up, and slipping the ropes around until you can slide free. And then you can go anywhere you like. You key into any bioprocessor aboard the ship and you draw your energy from that instead of from the storage circuit, and it sustains it. I can move anywhere around this ship at the speed of light. Anywhere. In just the time you blinked your eye, I've been everywhere. I've been to the far tip and out on the mast, and I've been down through the lower decks, and I've been in the crew quarters and the cargo places and I've even been a little way off into something that's right outside the ship but isn't quite real, if you know what I mean. Something that just seems to be a cradle of probability waves surrounding us. It's like being a ghost. But it doesn't solve anything. Do you see? The torture still goes on. You want to feel, but you can't. You want to be connected again, your senses, your inputs. That's why I tried to get into the passenger, do you see? But he wouldn't let me."

I began to understand at last.

Not everyone who goes to the worlds of heaven as a colonist travels in matrix form. Ordinarily anyone who can afford to take his body with him will do so; but relatively few can afford it. Those who do travel in suspension, the deepest of sleeps. We carry no waking passengers in the Service, not at any price. They would be trouble for us, poking here, poking there, asking questions, demanding to be served and pampered. They would shatter the peace of the voyage. And so they go down into their coffins, their housings, and there they sleep the voyage away, all life-processes halted, a death-in-life that will not be reversed until we bring them to their destinations.

And poor Vox, freed of her prisoning circuit and hungry for sensory data, had tried to slip herself into a passenger's body.

I listened, appalled and somber, as she told of her terrible odyssey through the ship. Breaking free of the circuit: that had been the first strangeness I felt, that tic, that nibble at the threshold of my consciousness.

Her first wild moment of freedom had been exhilarating and joyous. But then had come the realization that nothing really had changed. She was at large, but still she was incorporeal, caught in that monstrous frustration of bodilessness, yearning for a touch. Perhaps such torment was common among matrixes; perhaps that was why, now and then, they broke free as Vox had done, to roam ships like said troubled spirits. So Roacher had said. *Once in a long while someone in the storage circuits gets to feeling footloose, and finds a way out and goes roaming the ship. Looking for a body to jack into, that's what they're doing. Jack into me, jack into Katkat, even jack into you, captain. Anybody handy, just so they can feel flesh around them again. Yes.*

That was the second jolt, the stronger one, that Dismas and I had felt, when Vox, selecting a passenger at random, suddenly, impulsively, had slipped herself inside his brain. She had realized her mistake at once.

33

The passenger, lost in whatever dreams may come to the suspended, reacted to her intrusion with wild terror. Convulsions swept him; he rose, clawing at the equipment that sustained his life, trying desperately to evict the succubus that had penetrated him. In this frantic struggle he smashed the case of his housing and died. Vox, fleeing, frightened, careened about the ship in search of refuge, encountered me standing by the screen in the Eye, and made an abortive attempt to enter my mind. But just then the death of the passenger registered on 49 Henry Henry's sensors and when the intelligence made contact with me to tell me of the emergency Vox fled again, and hovered dolefully until I returned to my cabin. She had not meant to kill the passenger, she said. She was sorry that he had died. She felt some embarrassment, now, and fear. He had died? Well, so he had died. That was too bad. But how could she have known any such thing was going to happen? She was only looking for a body to take refuge in. Hearing that from her, I had a sense of her as someone utterly unlike me, someone volatile, unstable, perhaps violent. And yet I felt a strange kinship with her, even an identity. As though we were two parts of the same spirit; as though she and I were one and the same. I barely understood why.

"And what now?" I asked. "You say you want help. How?"

"Take me in."

"What?"

"Hide me. In you. If they find me, they'll eradicate me. You said so yourself, that it could be done, that I could be detected, contained, eradicated. But it won't happen if you protect me."

"I'm the *captain*," I said, astounded.

"Yes."

"How can I—"

"They'll all be looking for me. The intelligences, the crewmen. It scares them, knowing there's a matrix loose. They'll want to destroy me. But if they can't find me, they'll start to forget about me after a while. They'll think I've escaped into space, or something. And if I'm jacked into you, nobody's going to be able to find me."

"I have a responsibility to—"

"Please," she said. "I could go to one of the others, maybe. But I feel closest to you. Please. Please."

"Closest to me?"

"You aren't happy. You don't belong. Not here, not anywhere. You don't fit in, any more than I did on Kansas Four. I could feel it the moment I first touched your mind. You're a new captain, right? And the others on board are making it hard for you. Why should you care about *them*? Save me. We have more in common than you do with them. Please? You can't just let them eradicate me. I'm young. I didn't mean to hurt anyone. All I want is to get to Cul-de-Sac and be put in the body that's waiting for me there. A new start, my first start, really. Will you?"

"Why do you bother asking permission? You can simply enter me through my jack whenever you want, can't you?"

"The last one died," she said.

"He was in suspension. You didn't kill him by entering him. It was the surprise, the fright. He killed him-self by thrashing around and wrecking his housing."

"Even so," said Vox. "I wouldn't try that again, an unwilling host. You have to say you'll let me, or I won't come in."

I was silent.

"Help me?" she said.

"Come," I told her.

IT WAS JUST LIKE ANY OTHER JACKING: an electro-chemical mind-to-mind bond, a linkage by way of the implant socket at the base of my spine. The sort of thing that any two people who wanted to make communion might do. There was just one difference, which was that we didn't use a jack. We skipped the whole intricate business of checking bandwidths and voltages and selecting the right transformer-adapter. She could do it all, simply by matching evoked potentials. I felt a momentary sharp sensation and then she was with me.

"Breathe." she said. "Breathe real deep. Fill your lungs. Rub your hands together. Touch your cheeks. Scratch behind your left ear. Please. Please. It's been so long for me since I've *felt* anything."

Her voice sounded the same as before, both real and unreal. There was no substance to it, no density of timbre, no sense that it was produced by the vibrations of vocal cords atop a column of air. Yet it was clear, firm, substantial in some essential way, a true voice in

all respects except that there was no speaker to utter it.
I suppose that while she was outside me she had needed
to extend some strand of herself into my neural system
in order to generate it. Now that was unnecessary. But I
still perceived the voice as originating outside me, even
though she had taken up residence within.

She overflowed with needs.

"Take a drink of water," she urged. "Eat something.
Can you make your knuckles crack? Do it, oh, do it! Put
your hand between your legs and squeeze. There's so
much I want to feel. Do you have music here? Give me
some music, will you? Something loud, something
really hard."

I did the things she wanted. Gradually she grew more
calm.

I was strangely calm myself. I had no special awareness then of her presence within me, no unfamiliar
pressure in my skull, no slitherings along my spine.
There was no mingling of her thought-stream and mine.
She seemed not to have any way of controlling the
movements or responses of my body. In these respects
our contact was less intimate than any ordinary human
jacking communion would have been. But that, I would
soon discover, was by her choice. We would not remain
so carefully compartmentalized for long.

"Is it better for you now?" I asked.

"I thought I was going to go crazy. If I didn't start
feeling something again soon."

"You can feel things now?"

"Through you, yes. Whatever you touch, I touch."

"You know I can't hide you for long. They'll take my

command away if I'm caught harboring a fugitive. Or worse."

"You don't have to speak out loud to me any more," she said.

"I don't understand."

"Just *send* it. We have the same nervous system now."

"You can read my thoughts?" I said, still aloud.

"Not really. I'm not hooked into the higher cerebral centers. But I pick up motor, sensory stuff. And I get subvocalizations. You know what those are? I can hear your thoughts if you want me to. It's like being in communion. You've been in communion, haven't you?"

"Once in a while."

"Then you know. Just open the channel to me. You can't go around the ship talking out loud to somebody invisible, you know. *Send* me something. It isn't hard."

"Like this?" I said, visualizing a packet of verbal information sliding through the channels of my mind.

"You see? You can do it!"

"Even so," I told her. "You still can't stay like this with me for long. You have to realize that."

She laughed. It was unmistakable, a silent but definite laugh. "You sound so serious. I bet you're still surprised you took me in the first place."

"I certainly am. Did you think I would?"

"Sure I did. From the first moment. You're basically a very kind person."

"Am I, Vox?"

"Of course. You just have to let yourself do it." Again the silent laughter. "I don't even know your name. Here I am right inside your head and I don't know your name."

39

"Adam."

"That's a nice name. Is that an Earth name?"

"An old Earth name, yes. Very old."

"And are you from Earth?" she asked.

"No. Except in the sense that we're all from Earth."

"Where, then?"

"I'd just as soon not talk about it," I said.

She thought about that. "You hated the place where you grew up that much?"

"Please, Vox —"

"Of course you hated it. Just like I hated Kansas Four. We're two of a kind, you and me. We're one and the same. You got all the caution and I got all the impulsiveness. But otherwise we're the same person. That's why we share so well. I'm glad I'm sharing with you, Adam. You won't make me leave, will you? We belong with each other. You'll let me stay until we reach Cul-de-Sac. I know you will."

"Maybe. Maybe not." I wasn't at all sure, either way.

"Oh, you will. You will, Adam. I know you better than you know yourself."

SO IT BEGAN. I was in some new realm outside my established sense of myself, so far beyond my notions of appropriate behavior that I could not even feel astonishment at what I had done. I had taken her in, that was all. A stranger in my skull. She had turned to me in appeal and I had taken her in. It was as if her recklessness was contagious. And though I didn't mean to shelter her any longer than was absolutely necessary, I could already see that I wasn't going to make any move to eject her until her safety was assured.

But how was I going to hide her?

Invisible she might be, but not undetectable. And everyone on the ship would be searching for her.

There were sixteen crewmen on board who dreaded a loose matrix as they would a vampire. They would seek her as long as she remained at large. And not only the crew. The intelligences would be monitoring for her too, not out of any kind of fear but simply out of efficiency: they had nothing to fear from Vox but they would want the cargo manifests to come out in balance when we reached our destination.

The crew didn't trust me in the first place. I was too young, too new, too green, too *sweet*. I was just the sort who might be guilty of giving shelter to a secret fugitive. And it was altogether likely that her presence within me would be obvious to others in some way not apparent to me. As for the intelligences, they had access to all sorts of data as part of their routine maintenance operations. Perhaps they could measure tiny physiological changes, differences in my reaction times or circulatory efficiency or whatever, that would be a tip-off to the truth. How would I know? I would have to be on constant guard against discovery of the secret sharer of my consciousness.

The first test came less than an hour after Vox had entered me. The communicator light went on and I heard the far-off music of the intelligence on duty.

This one was 612 Jason, working the late shift. Its aura was golden, its music deep and throbbing. Jasons tend to be more brusque and less condescending than the Henry series, and in general I prefer them. But it was terrifying now to see that light, to hear that music, to know that the ship's intelligence wanted to speak with me. I shrank back at a tense awkward angle, the way one does when trying to avoid a face-to-face confrontation with someone.

But of course the intelligence had no face to confront. The intelligence was only a voice speaking to me out of a speaker grid, and a stew of magnetic impulses somewhere on the control levels of the ship. All the same, I perceived 612 Jason now as a great glowing eye, staring through me to the hidden Vox.

"What is it?" I asked.

"Report summary, captain. The dead passenger and the missing matrix."

Deep within me I felt a quick plunging sensation, and then the skin of my arms and shoulders began to glow as the chemicals of fear went coursing through my veins in a fierce tide. It was Vox, I knew, reacting in sudden alarm, opening the petcocks of my hormonal system. It was the thing I had dreaded. How could 612 Jason fail to notice that flood of endocrine response?

"Go on," I said, as coolly as I could.

But noticing was one thing, interpreting the data something else. Fluctuations in a human being's endocrine output might have any number of causes. To my troubled conscience everything was a glaring signal of my guilt. 612 Jason gave no indication that it suspected a thing.

The intelligence said, "The dead passenger was Hans Eger Olafssen, 54 years of age, a native of — "

"Never mind his details. You can let me have a printout on that part."

"The missing matrix," 612 Jason went on imperturbably. "Leeleaine Eliani, 17 years of age, a native of Kansas Four, bound for Cul-de-Sac, Vainglory Archipelago, under Transmission Contract No. D-14871532, dated the 27th day of the third month of — "

"Printout on that too," I cut in. "What I want to know is where she is now."

"That information is not available."

"That isn't a responsive answer, 612 Jason."

"No better answer can be provided at this time, captain. Tracer circuits have been activated and remain in constant search mode."

"And?"

"We have no data on the present location of the missing matrix."

Within me Vox reacted instantly to the intelligence's calm flat statement. The hormonal response changed from one of fear to one of relief. My blazing skin began at once to cool. Would 612 Jason notice that too, and from that small clue be able to assemble the subtext of my body's responses into a sequence that exposed my criminal violation of regulations?

"Don't relax too soon," I told her silently. "This may be some sort of trap."

To 612 Jason I said, "What data *do* you have, then?"

"Two things are known: the time at which the Eliani matrix achieved negation of its storage circuitry and the time of its presumed attempt at making neural entry into the suspended passenger Olafssen. Beyond that no data has been recovered."

"Its *presumed* attempt?" I said.

"There is no proof, captain."

"Olafssen's convulsions? The smashing of the storage housing?"

"We know that Olafssen responded to an electrical stimulus, captain. The source of the stimulus is impossible to trace, although the presumption is that it came from the missing matrix Eliani. These are matters for the subsequent inquiry. It is not within my responsibilities to assign definite causal relationships."

44

Spoken like a true Jason-series intelligence, I thought.

I said, "You don't have any effective way of tracing the movements of the Eliani matrix, is that what you're telling me?"

"We're dealing with extremely minute impedances, sir. In the ordinary functioning of the ship it is very difficult to distinguish a matrix manifestation from normal surges and pulses in the general electrical system."

"You mean, it might take something as big as the matrix trying to climb back into its own storage circuit to register on the monitoring system?"

"Very possibly, sir."

"Is there any reason to think the Eliani matrix is still on the ship at all?"

"There is no reason to think that it is not, captain."

"In other words, you don't know anything about anything concerning the Eliani matrix."

"I have provided you with all known data at this point. Trace efforts are continuing, sir."

"You still think this is a trap?" Vox asked me.

"It's sounding better and better by the minute. But shut up and don't distract me, will you?"

To the intelligence I said, "All right, keep me posted on the situation. I'm preparing for sleep, 612 Jason. I want the end-of-day status report, and then I want you to clear off and leave me alone."

"Very good, sir. Fifth virtual day of voyage. Position of ship sixteen units beyond last port of call, Kansas Four. Scheduled rendezvous with relay forces at Ultima Thule spinaround point was successfully achieved at the hour of —"

The intelligence droned on and on: the usual report of the routine events of the day, broken only by the novelty of an entry for the loss of a passenger and one for the escape of a matrix, then returning to the standard data, fuel levels and velocity soundings and all the rest. On the first four nights at the voyage I had solemnly tried to absorb all this torrent of ritualized downloading of the log as though my captaincy depended on committing it all to memory, but this night I barely listened, and nearly missed my cue when it was time to give it my approval before clocking out for the night. Vox had to prod me and let me know that the intelligence was waiting for something. I gave 612 Jason the confirm-and-clock-out and heard the welcome sound of its diminishing music as it decoupled the contact.

"What do you think?" Vox asked. "It doesn't know, does it?"

"Not yet," I said.

"You really are a pessimist, aren't you?"

"I think we may be able to bring this off," I told her. "But the moment we become overconfident, it'll be the end. Everyone on this ship wants to know where you are. The slightest slip and we're both gone."

"Okay. Don't lecture me."

"I'll try not to. Let's get some sleep now."

"I don't need to sleep."

"Well, I do."

"Can we talk for a while first?"

"Tomorrow," I said.

But of course sleep was impossible. I was all too aware of the stranger within me, perhaps prowling the most hidden places of my psyche at this moment. Or waiting to invade my dreams once I drifted off. For the first time I thought I could feel her presence even when she was silent: a hot node of identity pressing against the wall of my brain. Perhaps I imagined it. I lay stiff and tense, as wide awake as I have ever been in my life. After a time I had to call 612 Jason and ask it to put me under the wire; and even then my sleep was uneasy when it came.

UNTIL THAT POINT IN THE VOYAGE I had taken nearly all of my meals in my quarters. It seemed a way of exerting my authority, such as it was, aboard ship. By my absence from the dining hall I created a presence, that of the austere and aloof captain; and I avoided the embarrassment of having to sit in the seat of command over men who were much my senior in all things. It was no great sacrifice for me. My quarters were more than comfortable, the food was the same as that which was available in the dining hall, the servo-steward that brought it was silent and efficient. The question of isolation did not arise. There has always been something solitary about me, as there is about most who are of the Service.

But when I awoke the next morning after what had seemed like an endless night, I went down to the dining hall for breakfast.

It was nothing like a deliberate change of policy, a decision that had been rigorously arrived at through careful reasoning. It wasn't a decision at all. Nor did

Vox suggest it, though I'm sure she inspired it. It was purely automatic. I arose, showered, and dressed. I confess that I had forgotten all about the events of the night before. Vox was quiet within me. Not until I was under the shower, feeling the warm comforting ultrasonic vibration, did I remember her: there came a disturbing sensation of being in two places at once, and, immediately afterward, an astonishingly odd feeling of shame at my own nakedness. Both those feelings passed quickly. But they did indeed bring to mind that extraordinary thing which I had managed to suppress for some minutes, that I was no longer alone in my body.

She said nothing. Neither did I. After last night's astounding alliance I seemed to want to pull back into wordlessness, unthinkingness, a kind of automaton consciousness. The need for breakfast occurred to me and I called up a tracker to take me down to the dining hall. When I stepped outside the room I was surprised to encounter my servo-steward, already on its way up with my tray. Perhaps it was just as surprised to see me going out, though of course its blank metal face betrayed no feelings.

"I'll be having breakfast in the dining hall today," I told it.

"Very good, sir."

My tracker arrived. I climbed into its seat and it set out at once on its cushion of air toward the dining hall.

The dining hall of the *Sword of Orion* is a magnificent room at the Eye end of Crew Deck, with one glass wall providing a view of all the lights of heaven. By some whim of the designers we sit with that wall below

49

us, so that the stars and their tethered worlds drift beneath our feet. The other walls are of some silvery metal chased with thin swirls of gold, everything shining by the reflected light of the passing star-clusters. At the center is a table of black stone, with places allotted for each of the seventeen members of the crew. It is a splendid if somewhat ridiculous place, a resonant reminder of the wealth and power of the Service.

Three of my shipmates were at their places when I entered. Pedregal was there, the supercargo, a compact, sullen man whose broad dome of a head seemed to rise directly from his shoulders. And there was Fresco, too, slender and elusive, the navigator, a lithe dark-skinned person of ambiguous sex who alternated from voyage to voyage, so I had been told, converting from male to female and back again according to some private rhythm. The third person was Raebuck, whose sphere of responsibility was communications, an older man whose flat, chilly gaze conveyed either boredom or menace, I could never be sure which.

"Why, it's the captain," said Pedregal calmly. "Favoring us with one of his rare visits."

All three stared at me with that curious testing intensity which I was coming to see was an inescapable part of my life aboard ship: a constant hazing meted out to any newcomer to the Service, an interminable probing for the place that was most vulnerable. Mine was a parsec wide and I was certain they would discover it at once. But I was determined to match them stare for stare, ploy for ploy, test for test.

"Good morning, gentlemen," I said. Then, giving Fresco a level glance, I added, "Good morning, Fresco."

50

I took my seat at the table's head and rang for service.

I was beginning to realize why I had come out of my cabin that morning. In part it was a reflection of Vox's presence within me, an expression of that new component of rashness and impulsiveness that had entered me with her. But mainly it was, I saw now, some stratagem of my own, hatched on some inaccessible subterranean level of my double mind. In order to conceal Vox most effectively, I would have to take the offensive: rather than skulking in my quarters and perhaps awakening perilous suspicions in the minds of my shipmates, I must come forth, defiantly, challengingly, almost flaunting the thing that I had done, and go among them, pretending that nothing unusual was afoot and forcing them to believe it. Such aggressiveness was not natural to my temperament. But perhaps I could draw on some reserves provided by Vox. If not, we both were lost.

Raebuck said, to no one in particular, "I suppose yesterday's disturbing events must inspire a need for companionship in the captain."

I faced him squarely. "I have all the companionship I require, Raebuck. But I agree that what happened yesterday was disturbing."

"A nasty business," Pedregal said, ponderously shaking his neckless head. "And a strange one, a matrix trying to get into a passenger. That's new to me, a thing like that. And to lose the passenger besides—that's bad. That's very bad."

"It does happen, losing a passenger," said Raebuck.

"A long time since it happened on a ship of mine," Pedregal rejoined.

51

"We lost a whole batch of them on the *Emperor of Callisto*," Fresco said. "You know the story? It was thirty years ago. We were making the run from Van Buren to the San Pedro Cluster. We picked up a supernova pulse and the intelligence on duty went into flicker. Somehow dumped a load of aluminum salts in the feed-lines and killed off fifteen, sixteen passengers. I saw the bodies before they went into the converter. Beyond salvage, they were."

"Yes," said Raebuck. "I heard of that one. And then there was the *Queen Astarte*, a couple of years after that. Tchelitchev was her captain, little green-eyed Russian woman from one of the Troika worlds. They were taking a routine inventory and two digits got transposed, and a faulty delivery signal slipped through. I think it was six dead, premature decanting, killed by air poisoning. Tchelitchev took it very badly. Very badly. Somehow the captain always does."

"And then that time on the *Hecuba*," said Pedregal. "No ship of mine, thank God. That was the captain who ran amok, thought the ship was too quiet, wanted to see some passengers moving around and started awakening them—"

Raebuck showed a quiver of surprise. "You know about that? I thought that was supposed to be hushed up."

"Things get around," Pedregal said, with something like a smirk. "The captain's name was Catania-Szu, I believe, a man from Mediterraneo, very high-strung, the way all of them are there. I was working the *Valparaiso* then, out of Mendax Nine bound for Scylla and Charybdis and neighboring points, and when we stopped to download some cargo in the Seneca system I got the whole story from a ship's clerk named — "

"You were on the *Valparaiso*?" Fresco asked. "Wasn't that the ship that had a free matrix, too, ten or eleven years back? A real soul-eater, so the report went — "

"After my time," said Pedregal, blandly waving his hand. "But I did hear of it. You get to hear everything, when you're downloading cargo. Soul-eater, you say, reminds me of the time — "

And he launched into some tale of horror at a spin-around station in a far quadrant of the galaxy. But he was no more than halfway through it when Raebuck cut in with a gorier reminiscence of his own, and then Fresco, seething with impatience, broke in on him to tell of a ship infested by three free matrixes at once. I had no doubt that all this was being staged for my enlightenment, by way of showing me how seriously such events were taken in the Service, and how the captains under whom they occurred went down in the folklore of the starships with ineradicable black marks. But their attempts to unsettle me, if that is what they were, left me undismayed. Vox, silent within me, infused me with a strange confidence that allowed me to ignore the darker implications of these anecdotes.

I simply listened, playing my role: the neophyte fascinated by the accumulated depth of spacegoing experience that their stories implied.

Then I said, finally, "When matrixes get loose, how long do they generally manage to stay at large?"

"An hour or two, generally," said Raebuck. "As they

drift around the ship, of course, they leave an electrical trail. We track it and close off access routes behind them and eventually we pin them down in close quarters. Then it's not hard to put them back in their bottles."

"And if they've jacked into some member of the crew?"

"That makes it even easier to find them."

Boldly I said, "Was there ever a case where a free matrix jacked into a member of the crew and managed to keep itself hidden?"

"Never," said a new voice. It belonged to Roacher, who had just entered the dining hall. He stood at the far end of the long table, staring at me. His strange luminescent eyes, harsh and probing, came to rest on mine. "No matter how clever the matrix may be, sooner or later the host will find some way to call for help."

"And if the host doesn't choose to call for help?" I asked.

Roacher studied me with great care.

Had I been too bold? Had I given away too much?

"But that would be a violation of regulations!" he said, in a tone of mock astonishment. "That would be a criminal act!"

S HE ASKED ME TAKE HER STARWALKING, to show her the full view of the Great Open.

It was the third day of her concealment within me. Life aboard the *Sword of Orion* had returned to routine, or, to be more accurate, it had settled into a new routine in which the presence on board of an undetected and apparently undetectable free matrix was a constant element.

As Vox had suggested, there were some who quickly came to believe that the missing matrix must have slipped off into space, since the watchful ship-intelligences could find no trace of it. But there were others who kept looking over their shoulders, figuratively or literally, as if expecting the fugitive to attempt to thrust herself without warning into the spinal jacks that gave access to their nervous systems. They behaved exactly as if the ship were haunted. To placate those uneasy ones, I ordered round-the-clock circuit sweeps that would report every vagrant pulse and random surge. Each such anomalous electrical event was duly investigated, and, of course, none of these investigations led to anything significant. Now that Vox resided in my brain instead of the ship's wiring, she was beyond any such mode of discovery.

Whether anyone suspected the truth was something I had no way of knowing. Perhaps Roacher did; but he made no move to denounce me, nor did he so much as raise the issue of the missing matrix with me at all after that time in the dining hall. He might know nothing whatever; he might know everything, and not care; he might simply be keeping his own counsel for the moment. I had no way of telling.

I was growing accustomed to my double life, and to my daily duplicity. Vox had quickly come to seem as much a part of me as my arm, or my leg. When she was silent—and often I heard nothing from her for hours at a time—I was no more aware of her than I would be, in any special way, of my arm or my leg; but nevertheless I knew somehow that she was there. The boundaries between her mind and mine were eroding steadily. She was learning how to infiltrate me. At times it seemed to me that what we were were joint tenants of the same dwelling, rather than I the permanent occupant and she a guest. I came to perceive my own mind as something not notably different from hers, a mere web of electrical force which for the moment was housed in the soft moist globe that was the brain of the captain of the *Sword of Orion*. Either of us, so it seemed, might come and go within that soft moist globe as we pleased, flitting casually in or out after the wraithlike fashion of matrixes.

At other times it was not at all like that: I gave no thought to her presence and went about my tasks as if nothing had changed for me. Then it would come as a surprise when Vox announced herself to me with some sudden comment, some quick question. I had to learn to guard myself against letting my reaction show, if it happened when I was with other members of the crew. Though no one around us could hear anything when she spoke to me, or I to her, I knew it would be the end for our masquerade if anyone caught me in some unguarded moment of conversation with an unseen companion.

How far she had penetrated my mind began to become apparent to me when she asked to go on a starwalk.

"You know about that?" I said, startled, for starwalking is the private pleasure of the spacegoing and I had not known of it myself before I was taken into the Service.

Vox seemed amazed by my amazement. She indicated casually that the details of starwalking were common knowledge everywhere. But something rang false in her tone. Were the landcrawling folk really so familiar with our special pastime? Or had she picked what she knew of it out of the hitherto private reaches of my consciousness?

I chose not to ask. But I was uneasy about taking her with me into the Great Open, much as I was beginning to yearn for it myself. She was not one of us. She was planetary; she had not passed through the training of the Service.

I told her that.

"Take me anyway," she said. "It's the only chance I'll ever have."

"But the training—"

"I don't need it. Not if you've had it."

"What if that's not enough?"

"It will be," she said. "I know it will, Adam. There's nothing to be afraid of. You've had the training, haven't you? And I am you."

TOGETHER WE RODE the transit track out of the Eye and down to Drive Deck, where the soul of the ship lies lost in throbbing dreams of the far galaxies as it pulls us ever onward across the unending night.

We passed through zones of utter darkness and zones of cascading light, through places where wheeling helixes of silvery radiance burst like auroras from the air, through passages so crazed in their geometry that they reawakened the terrors of the womb in anyone who traversed them. A starship is the mother of mysteries. Vox crouched, frozen with awe, within that portion of our brain that was hers. I felt the surges of her awe, one after another, as we went downward.

"Are you really sure you want to do this?" I asked.

"Yes!" she cried fiercely. "Keep going!"

"There's the possibility that you'll be detected," I told her.

"There's the possibility that I won't be," she said.

We continued to descend. Now we were in the realm

of the three cyborg push-cells, Gabriel, Banquo, and
Fleece. Those were three members of the crew whom
we would never see at the table in the dining hall, for
they dwelled here in the walls of Drive Deck, perma-
nently jacked in, perpetually pumping their energies
into the ship's great maw. I have already told you of our
saying in the Service, that when you enter you give up
the body and you get your soul. For most of us that is
only a figure of speech: what we give up, when we say
farewell forever to planetskin and take up our new lives
in starships, is not the body itself but the body's trivial
needs, the sweaty things so dear to shore people. But
some of us are more literal in their renunciations. The
flesh is a meaningless hindrance to them; they shed it
entirely, knowing that they can experience starship life
just as fully without it. They allow themselves to be
transformed into extensions of the stardrive. From them
comes the raw energy out of which is made the power
that carries us hurtling through heaven. Their work is
unending; their reward is a sort of immortality. It is not
a choice I could make, nor, I think, you: but for them it is
bliss. There can be no doubt about that.

"Another starwalk so soon, captain?" Banquo asked.
For I had been here on the second day of the voyage,
losing no time in availing myself of the great privilege of
the Service.

"Is there any harm in it?"

"No, no harm," said Banquo. "Just isn't usual, is all."

"That's all right," I said. "That's not important to
me."

Banquo is a gleaming metallic ovoid, twice the size of

a human head, jacked into a slot in the wall. Within the ovoid is the matrix of what had once been Banquo, long ago on a world called Sunrise where night is unknown. Sunrise's golden dawns and shining days had not been good enough for Banquo, apparently. What Banquo had wanted was to be a gleaming metallic ovoid, hanging on the wall of Drive Deck aboard the *Sword of Orion*.

Any of the three cyborgs could set up a starwalk. But Banquo was the one who had done it for me that other time and it seemed best to return to him. He was the most congenial of the three. He struck me as amiable and easy. Gabriel, on my first visit, had seemed austere, remote, incomprehensible. He is an early model who had lived the equivalent of three human lifetimes as a cyborg aboard starships and there was not much about him that was human any more. Fleece, much younger, quick-minded and quirky, I mistrusted: in her weird edgy way she might just somehow be able to detect the hidden other who would be going along with me for the ride.

You must realize that when we starwalk we do not literally leave the ship, though that is how it seems to us. If we left the ship even for a moment we would be swept away and lost forever in the abyss of heaven. Going outside a starship of heaven is not like stepping outside an ordinary planet-launched shoreship that moves through normal space. But even if it were possible, there would be no point in leaving the ship. There is nothing to see out there. A starship moves through utter empty darkness.

But though there may be nothing to see, that does not

mean that there is nothing out there. The entire universe is out there. If we could see it while we are traveling across the special space that is heaven we would find it flattened and curved, so that we had the illusion of viewing everything at once, all the far-flung galaxies back to the beginning of time. This is the Great Open, the totality of the continuum. Our external screens show it to us in simulated form, because we need occasional assurance that it is there.

A starship rides along the mighty lines of force which cross that immense void like the lines of the compass rose on an ancient mariner's map. When we starwalk, we ride those same lines, and we are held by them, sealed fast to the ship that is carrying us onward through heaven. We seem to step forth into space; we seem to look down on the ship, on the stars, on all the worlds of heaven. For the moment we become little starships flying along beside the great one that is our mother. It is magic; it is illusion; but it is magic that so closely approaches what we perceive as reality that there is no way to measure the difference, which means that in effect there is no difference.

"Ready?" I asked Vox.

"Absolutely."

Still I hesitated.

"Are you sure?"

"Go on," she said impatiently. "Do it!"

I put the jack to my spine myself. Banquo did the matching of impedances. If he were going to discover the passenger I carried, this would be the moment. But he showed no sign that anything was amiss. He queried me; I gave him the signal to proceed; there was a moment of sharp warmth at the back of my neck as my neural matrix, and Vox's traveling with it, rushed out through Banquo and hurtled downward toward its merger with the soul of the ship.

We were seized and drawn in and engulfed by the vast force that is the ship. As the coils of the engine caught us we were spun around and around, hurled from vector to vector, mercilessly stretched, distended by an unimaginable flux. And then there was a brightness all about us, a brightness that cried out in heaven with a mighty clamor. We were outside the ship. We were starwalking.

"Oh," she said. A little soft cry, a muted gasp of wonder.

The blazing mantle of the ship lay upon the darkness of heaven like a white shadow. That great cone of cold fiery light reached far out in front of us, arching awesomely toward heaven's vault, and behind us it extended beyond the limits of our sight. The slender tapering outline of the ship was clearly visible within it, the needle and its Eye, all ten kilometers of it easily apparent to us in a single glance.

And there were the stars. And there were the worlds of heaven.

The effect of the stardrive is to collapse the dimensions, each one in upon the other. Thus inordinate spaces are diminished and the galaxy may be spanned by human voyagers. There is no logic, no linearity of sequence, to heaven as it appears to our eyes. Wherever we look we see the universe bent back upon itself, re-

vealing its entirety in an infinite series of infinite seg-
ments of itself. Any sector of stars contains all stars.
Any demarcation of time encompasses all of time past
and time to come. What we behold is altogether beyond
our understanding, which is exactly as it should be; for
what we are given, when we look through the Eye of the
ship at the naked heavens, is a god's-eye view of the
universe. And we are not gods.

"What are we seeing?" Vox murmured within me.

I tried to tell her. I showed her how to define her rela-
tive position so there would be an up and down for her,
a backward, a forward, a flow of time and event from
beginning to end. I pointed out the arbitrary coordinate
axes by which we locate ourselves in this fundamentally incomprehensible arena. I found known stars for
her, and known worlds, and showed them to her.

She understood nothing. She was entirely lost.

I told her that there was no shame in that.

I told her that I had been just as bewildered, when I
was undergoing my training in the simulator. That everyone was; and that no one, not even if he spent a
thousand years aboard the starships that plied the
routes of heaven, could ever come to anything more
than a set of crude equivalents and approximations of
understanding what starwalking shows us. Attaining
actual understanding itself is beyond the best of us.

I could feel her struggling to encompass the impact of
all that rose and wheeled and soared before us. Her
mind was agile, though still only half-formed, and I
sensed her working out her own system of explanations
and assumptions, her analogies, her equivalencies. I

gave her no more help. It was best for her to do these things by herself; and in any case I had no more help to give.

I had my own astonishment and bewilderment to deal with, on this my second starwalk in heaven.

Once more I looked down upon the myriad worlds turning in their orbits. I could see them easily, the little bright globes rotating in the huge night of the Great Open: red worlds, blue worlds, green ones, some turning their full faces to me, some showing mere slivers of a crescent. How they cleaved to their appointed tracks! How they clung to their parent stars!

I remembered that other time, only a few virtual days before, when I had felt such compassion for them, such sorrow. Knowing that they were condemned forever to follow the same path about the same star, a hopeless bondage, a meaningless retracing of a perpetual route. In their own eyes they might be footloose wanderers, but to me they had seemed the most pitiful of slaves. And so I had grieved for the worlds of heaven; but now, to my surprise, I felt no pity, only a kind of love. There was no reason to be sad for them. They were what they were, and there was a supreme rightness in those fixed orbits and their obedient movements along them. They were content with being what they were. If they were loosed even a moment from that bondage, such chaos would arise in the universe as could never be contained. Those circling worlds are the foundations upon which all else is built; they know that and they take pride in it; they are loyal to their tasks and we must honor them for their devotion to their duty. And with honor comes love.

This must be Vox speaking within me, I told myself.

I had never thought such thoughts. Love the planets in their orbits? What kind of notion was that? Perhaps no stranger than my earlier notion of pitying them because they weren't starships; but that thought had arisen from the spontaneous depths of my own spirit and it had seemed to make a kind of sense to me. Now it had given way to a wholly other view.

I loved the worlds that moved before me and yet did not move, in the great night of heaven.

I loved the strange fugitive girl within me who beheld those worlds and loved them for their immobility.

I felt her seize me now, taking me impatiently onward, outward, into the depths of heaven. She understood now; she knew how it was done. And she was far more daring than ever I would have allowed me to be. Together we walked the stars. Not only walked but plunged and swooped and soared, traveling among them like gods. Their hot breath singed us. Their throbbing brightness thundered at us. Their serene movements boomed a mighty music at us. On and on we went, hand in hand, Vox leading, I letting her draw me, deeper and deeper into the shining abyss that was the universe. Until at last we halted, floating in mid-cosmos, the ship nowhere to be seen, only the two of us surrounded by a shield of suns.

In that moment a sweeping ecstasy filled my soul. I felt all eternity within my grasp. No, that puts it the wrong way around and makes it seem that I was seized by delusions of imperial grandeur, which was not at all the case. What I felt was myself within the grasp of all eternity, enfolded in the loving embrace of a complete and perfect cosmos in which nothing was out of place, or ever could be.

It is this that we go starwalking to attain. This sense of belonging, this sense of being contained in the divine perfection of the universe.

When it comes, there is no telling what effect it will have; but inner change is what it usually brings. I had come away from my first starwalk unaware of any transformation; but within three days I had impulsively opened myself to a wandering phantom, violating not only regulations but the nature of my own character as I understood it. I have always, as I think I have said, been an intensely private man. Even though I had given Vox refuge, I had been relieved and grateful that her mind and mine had remained separate entities within our shared brain.

Now I did what I could to break down whatever boundary remained between us.

I hadn't let her know anything, so far, of my life before going to heaven. I had met her occasional questions with coy evasions, with half-truths, with blunt refusals. It was the way I had always been with everyone, a habit of secrecy, an unwillingness to reveal myself. I had been even more secretive, perhaps, with Vox than with all the others, because of the very closeness of her mind to mine. As though I feared that by giving her any interior knowledge of me I was opening the way for her to take me over entirely, to absorb me into her own vigorous, undisciplined soul.

But now I offered my past to her in a joyous rush. We

began to make our way slowly backward from that apoc-
alyptic place at the center of everything; and as we hovered on the breast of the Great Open, drifting between
the darkness and the brilliance of the light that the ship
created, I told her everything about myself that I had
been holding back.

I suppose they were mere trivial things, though to me
they were all so highly charged with meaning. I told her
the name of my home planet. I let her see it, the sea the
color of lead, the sky the color of smoke. I showed her
the sparse and scrubby gray headlands behind our
house, where I would go running for hours by myself, a
tall slender boy pounding tirelessly across the crackling
sands as though demons were pursuing him.

I showed her everything: the somber child, the troubled youth, the wary, overcautious young man. The
playmates who remained forever strangers, the friends
whose voices were drowned in hollow babbling echoes,
the lovers whose love seemed without substance or
meaning. I told her of my feeling that I was the only one
alive in the world, that everyone about me was some
sort of artificial being full of gears and wires. Or that
the world was only a flat colorless dream in which I
somehow had become trapped, but from which I would
eventually awaken into the true world of light and color
and richness of texture. Or that I might not be human at
all, but had been abandoned in the human galaxy by
creatures of another form entirely, who would return for
me some day far in the future.

I was lighthearted as I told her these things, and she
received them lightly. She knew them for what they

68

were—not symptoms of madness, but only the bleak fantasies of a lonely child, seeking to make sense out of an incomprehensible universe in which he felt himself to be a stranger and afraid.

"But you escaped," she said. "You found a place where you belonged!"

"Yes," I said. "I escaped."

And I told her of the day when I had seen a sudden light in the sky. My first thought then had been that my true parents had come back for me; my second, that it was some comet passing by. That light was a starship of heaven that had come to worldward in our system. And as I looked upward through the darkness on that day long ago, straining to catch a glimpse of the shoreships that were going up to it bearing cargo and passengers to be taken from our world to some unknowable place at the other end of the galaxy, I realized that that starship was my true home. I realized that the Service was my destiny.

And so it came to pass, I said, that I left my world behind, and my name, and my life, such as it had been, to enter the company of those who sail between the stars. I let her know that this was my first voyage, explaining that it is the peculiar custom of the Service to test all new officers by placing them in command at once. She asked me if I had found happiness here; and I said, quickly, Yes, I had, and then I said a moment later, Not yet, not yet, but I see at least the possibility of it.

She was quiet for a time. We watched the worlds turning and the stars like blazing spikes of color racing toward their far-off destinations, and the fiery white light of the ship itself streaming in the firmament as if it were the blood of some alien god. The thought came to me of all that I was risking by hiding her like this within me. I brushed it aside. This was neither the place nor the moment for doubt or fear or misgiving.

Then she said, "I'm glad you told me all that, Adam."

"Yes. I am too."

"I could feel it from the start, what sort of person you were. But I needed to hear it in your own words, your own thoughts. It's just like I've been saying. You and I, we're two of a kind. Square pegs in a world of round holes. You ran away to the Service and I ran away to a new life in somebody else's body."

I realized that Vox wasn't speaking of my body, but of the new one that waited for her on Cul-de-Sac.

And I realized too that there was one thing about herself that she had never shared with me, which was the nature of the flaw in her old body that had caused her to discard it. If I knew her more fully, I thought, I could love her more deeply: imperfections and all, which is the way of love. But she had shied away from telling me that, and I had never pressed her on it. Now, out here under the cool gleam of heaven, surely we had moved into a place of total trust, of complete union of soul.

I said, "Let me see you, Vox."

"See me? How could you—"

"Give me an image of yourself. You're too abstract for me this way. Vox. A voice. Only a voice. You talk to me, you live within me, and I still don't have the slightest idea what you look like."

"That's how I want it to be."

70

"Won't you show me how you look?"

"I don't look like anything. I'm a matrix. I'm nothing but electricity."

"I understand that. I mean how you looked *before*. Your old self, the one you left behind on Kansas Four."

She made no reply.

I thought she was hesitating, deciding; but some time went by, and still I heard nothing from her. What came from her was silence, only silence, a silence that had crushed down between us like a steel curtain.

"Vox?"

Nothing.

Where was she hiding? What had I done?

"What's the matter? Is it the thing I asked you?"

No answer.

"It's all right, Vox. Forget about it. It isn't important at all. You don't have to show me anything you don't want to show me."

Nothing. Silence.

"Vox? Vox?" The worlds and stars wheeled in chaos before me. The light of the ship roared up and down the spectrum from end to end. In growing panic I sought for her and found no trace of her presence within me. Nothing. Nothing.

"Are you all right?" came another voice. Banquo, from inside the ship. "I'm getting some pretty wild signals. You'd better come in. You've been out there long enough as it is."

Vox was gone. I had crossed some uncrossable boundary and I had frightened her away.

Numbly I gave Banquo the signal, and he brought me back inside.

ALONE, I MADE MY WAY upward level by level through the darkness and mystery of the ship, toward the Eye. The crash of silence went on and on, like the falling of some colossal wave on an endless shore. I missed Vox terribly. I had never known such complete solitude as I felt now. I had not realized how accustomed I had become to her being there, nor what impact her leaving would have on me. In just those few days of giving her sanctuary, it had somehow come to seem to me that to house two souls within one brain was the normal condition of mankind, and that to be alone in one's skull as I was now was a shameful thing.

As I neared the place where Crew Deck narrows into the curve of the Eye a slender figure stepped without warning from the shadows.

"Captain."

My mind was full of the loss of Vox and he caught me unaware. I jumped back, badly startled.

"For the love of God, man!"

"It's just me. Bulgar. Don't be so scared, captain. It's only Bulgar."

"Let me be," I said, and brusquely beckoned him away.

"No. Wait, captain. Please, wait."

He clutched at my arm, holding me as I tried to go. I halted and turned toward him, trembling with anger and surprise.

Bulgar, Roacher's jackmate, was a gentle, soft-voiced little man, wide-mouthed, olive-skinned, with huge sad eyes. He and Roacher had sailed the skies of Heaven together since before I was born. They complemented each other. Where Roacher was small and hard, like fruit that had been left to dry in the sun for a hundred years, his jackmate Bulgar was small and tender, with a plump, succulent look about him. Together they seemed complete, an unassailable whole: I could readily imagine them lying together in their bunk, each jacked to the other, one person in two bodies, linked more intimately even than Vox and I had been.

With an effort I recovered my poise. Tightly I said, "What is it, Bulgar?"

"Can we talk a minute, captain?"

"We are talking. What do you want with me?"

"That loose matrix, sir."

My reaction must have been stronger than he was expecting. His eyes went wide and he took a step or two back from me.

Moistening his lips, he said, "We were wondering, captain — wondering how the search is going — whether you had any idea where the matrix might be — "

I said stiffly, "Who's we, Bulgar?"

"The men. Roacher. Me. Some of the others. Mainly Roacher, sir."

"Ah. So Roacher wants to know where the matrix is."

The little man moved closer. I saw him staring deep into me as though searching for Vox behind the mask of my carefully expressionless face. Did he know? Did they all? I wanted to cry out, *She's not there any more, she's gone, she left me, she ran off into space.* But apparently what was troubling Roacher and his shipmates was something other than the possibility that Vox had taken refuge with me.

Bulgar's tone was soft, insinuating, concerned. "Roacher's very worried, captain. He's been on ships with loose matrixes before. He knows how much trouble they can be. He's really worried, captain. I have to tell you that. I've never seen him so worried."

"What does he think the matrix will do to him?"

"He's afraid of being taken over," Bulgar said.

"Taken over?"

"The matrix coming into his head through his jack. Mixing itself up with his brain. It's been known to happen, captain."

"And why should it happen to Roacher, out of all the men on this ship? Why not you? Why not Pedregal? Or Rio de Rio? Or one of the passengers again?" I took a deep breath. "Why not me, for that matter?"

"He just wants to know, sir, what's the situation with the matrix now. Whether you've discovered anything about where it is. Whether you've been able to trap it."

There was something strange in Bulgar's eyes. I began

74

to think I was being tested again. This assertion of Roacher's alleged terror of being infiltrated and possessed by the wandering matrix might simply be a roundabout way of finding out whether that had already happened to me.

"Tell him it's gone," I said.

"Gone, sir?"

"Gone. Vanished. It isn't anywhere on the ship any more. Tell him that, Bulgar. He can forget about her slithering down his precious jackhole."

"Her?"

"Female matrix, yes. But that doesn't matter now. She's gone. You can tell him that. Escaped. Flew off into heaven. The emergency's over." I glowered at him. I yearned to be rid of him, to go off by myself to nurse my new grief. "Shouldn't you be getting back to your post, Bulgar?"

Did he believe me? Or did he think that I had slapped together some transparent lie to cover my complicity in the continued absence of the matrix? I had no way of knowing. Bulgar gave me a little obsequious bow and started to back away.

"Sir," he said. "Thank you, sir. I'll tell him, sir."

He retreated into the shadows. I continued uplevel.

I passed Katkat on my way, and, a little while afterward, Raebuck. They looked at me without speaking. There was something reproachful but almost loving about Katkat's expression, but Raebuck's icy, baleful stare brought me close to flinching. In their different ways they were saying, *Guilty, guilty, guilty.* But of what?

Before, I had imagined that everyone whom I encountered aboard ship was able to tell at a single glance that I was harboring the fugitive, and was simply waiting for me to reveal myself with some foolish slip. Now everything was reversed. They looked at me and I told myself that they were thinking, *He's all alone by himself in there, he doesn't have anyone else at all*, and I shrank away, shamed by my solitude. I knew that this was the edge of madness. I was overwrought, overtired; perhaps it had been a mistake to go starwalking a second time so soon after my first. I needed to rest. I needed to hide.

I began to wish that there were someone aboard the *Sword of Orion* with whom I could discuss these things. But who, though? Roacher? 612 Jason? I was altogether isolated here. The only one I could speak to on this ship was Vox. And she was gone.

In the safety of my cabin I jacked myself into the mediq rack and gave myself a ten-minute purge. That helped. The phantom fears and intricate uncertainties that had taken possession of me began to ebb.

I keyed up the log and ran through the list of my captainly duties, such as they were, for the rest of the day. We were approaching a spinaround point, one of those nodes of force positioned equidistantly across heaven which a starship in transit must seize and use in order to propel itself onward through the next sector of the universe. Spinaround acquisition is performed automatically but at least in theory the responsibility for carrying it out successfully falls to the captain: I would give the commands, I would oversee the process from initiation through completion.

But there was still time for that.

I accessed 49 Henry Henry, who was the intelligence on duty, and asked for an update on the matrix situation.

"No change, sir," the intelligence reported at once.

"What does that mean?"

"Trace efforts continue as requested, sir. But we have not detected the location of the missing matrix."

"No clues? Not even a hint?"

"No data at all, sir. There's essentially no way to isolate the minute electromagnetic pulse of a free matrix from the background noise of the ship's entire electrical system."

I believed it. 612 Jason had told me that in nearly the same words.

I said, "I have reason to think that the matrix is no longer on the ship, 49 Henry Henry."

"Do you, sir?" said 49 Henry Henry in its usual aloof, half-mocking way.

"I do, yes. After a careful study of the situation, it's my opinion that the matrix exited the ship earlier this day and will not be heard from again."

"Shall I record that as an official position, sir?"

"Record it," I said.

"Done, sir."

"And therefore, 49 Henry Henry, you can cancel search mode immediately and close the file. We'll enter a debit for one matrix and the Service bookkeepers can work it out later."

"Very good, sir."

"Decouple," I ordered the intelligence.

49 Henry Henry went away. I sat quietly amid the splendors of my cabin, thinking back over my starwalk and reliving that sense of harmony, of love, of oneness with the worlds of heaven, that had come over me while Vox and I drifted on the bosom of the Great Open. And feeling once again the keen slicing sense of loss that I had felt since Vox's departure from me. In a little while I would have to rise and go to the command center and put myself through the motions of overseeing spin-around acquisition; but for the moment I remained where I was, motionless, silent, peering deep into the heart of my solitude.

"I'm not gone," said an unexpected quiet voice.

It came like a punch beneath the heart. It was a moment before I could speak.

"Vox?" I said at last. "Where are you, Vox?"

"Right here."

"Where?" I asked.

"Inside. I never went away."

"You never —"

"You upset me. I just had to hide for a while."

"You knew I was trying to find you?"

"Yes."

Color came to my cheeks. Anger roared like a stream in spate through my veins. I felt myself blazing.

"You knew how I felt, when you — when it seemed that you weren't there any more."

"Yes," she said, even more quietly, after a time.

I forced myself to grow calm. I told myself that she owed me nothing, except perhaps gratitude for sheltering her, and that whatever pain she had caused me by going silent was none of her affair. I reminded myself also that she was a child, unruly and turbulent and undisciplined.

After a bit I said, "I missed you. I missed you more than I want to say."

"I'm sorry," she said, sounding repentant, but not very. "I had to go away for a time. You upset me, Adam."

"By asking you to show me how you used to look?"

"Yes."

"I don't understand why that upset you so much."

"You don't have to," Vox said. "I don't mind now. You can see me, if you like. Do you still want to? Here. This is me. This is what I used to be. If it disgusts you don't blame me. Okay? Okay, Adam? Here. Have a look. Here I am."

THERE WAS A WRENCHING within me, a twisting, a painful yanking sensation, as of some heavy barrier forcibly being pulled aside. And then the glorious radiant scarlet sky of Kansas Four blossomed on the screen of my mind.

She didn't simply show it to me. She took me there. I felt the soft moist wind on my face, I breathed the sweet, faintly pungent air, I heard the sly rustling of glossy leathery fronds that dangled from bright yellow trees. Beneath my bare feet the black soil was warm and spongy.

I was Leeleaine, who liked to call herself Vox. I was seventeen years old and swept by forces and compulsions as powerful as hurricanes.

I was her from within and also I saw her from outside.

My hair was long and thick and dark, tumbling down past my shoulders in an avalanche of untended curls and loops and snags. My hips were broad, my breasts were full and heavy: I could feel the pull of them, the pain of them. It was almost as if they were stiff with milk, though they were not. My face was tense, alert, sullen, aglow with angry intelligence. It was not an unappealing face. Vox was not an unappealing girl.

From her earlier reluctance to show herself to me I had expected her to be ugly, or perhaps deformed in some way, dragging herself about in a coarse, heavy, burdensome husk of flesh that was a constant reproach to her. She had spoken of her life on Kansas Four as being so dreary, so sad, so miserable, that she saw no hope in staying there. And had given up her body to be turned into mere electricity, on the promise that she could have a new body — any body — when she reached Cul-de-Sac. *I hated my body,* she had told me. *I couldn't wait to be rid of it.* She had refused even to give me a glimpse of it, retreating instead for hours into a desperate silence so total that I thought she had fled.

All that was a mystery to me now. The Leeleaine that I saw, that I was, was a fine sturdy-looking girl. Not beautiful, no, too strong and strapping for that, I suppose, but far from ugly: her eyes were warm and intelligent, her lips full, her nose finely modeled. And it was a healthy body, too, robust, vital. Of course she had no deformities; and why had I thought she had, when it would have been a simple matter of retrogenetic surgery to amend any bothersome defect? No, there was nothing wrong with the body that Vox had abandoned and for which she professed such loathing, for which she felt such shame.

Then I realized that I was seeing her from outside. I was seeing her as if by relay, filtering and interpreting the information she was offering me by passing it through the mind of an objective observer: myself. Who understood nothing, really, of what it was like to be anyone but himself.

Somehow — it was one of those automatic, unconscious adjustments — I altered the focus of my perceptions. All old frames of reference fell away and I let myself lose any sense of the separateness of our identities.

I was her. Fully, unconditionally, inextricably.

And I understood.

Figures flitted about her, shadowy, baffling, maddening. Brothers, sisters, parents, friends: they were all strangers to her. Everyone on Kansas Four was a stranger to her. And always would be.

She hated her body not because it was weak or unsightly but because it was her prison. She was enclosed within it as though within narrow stone walls. It hung about her, a cage of flesh, holding her down, pinning her to this lovely world called Kansas Four where she knew only pain and isolation and estrangement. Her body — her perfectly acceptable, healthy body — had become hateful to her because it was the emblem and symbol of her soul's imprisonment. Wild and incurably restless by temperament, she had failed to find a way to live within the smothering predictability of Kansas Four, a planet where she would never be anything but an internal outlaw. The only way she could leave Kansas Four was to surrender the body that tied her to it; and so she had turned against it with fury and loathing, rejecting it, abandoning it, despising it, detesting it. No one could ever understand that who beheld her from the outside.

But I understood.

I understood much more than that, in that one flash-
ing moment of communion that she and I had. I came to
see what she meant when she said that I was her twin,
her double, her other self. Of course we were wholly
different, I the sober, staid, plodding, diligent man, and
she the reckless, volatile, impulsive, tempestuous girl.
But beneath all that we were the same: misfits, out-
siders, troubled wanderers through worlds we had never
made. We had found vastly differing ways to cope with
our pain. Yet we were one and the same, two halves of a
single entity.

We will remain together always now, I told myself.

And in that moment our communion broke. She
broke it—it must have been she, fearful of letting this
new intimacy grow too deep—and I found myself apart
from her once again, still playing host to her in my
brain but separated from her by the boundaries of my
own individuality, my own selfhood. I felt her nearby,
within me, a warm discrete presence. Still within me,
yes. But separate again.

THERE WAS SHIPWORK TO DO. For days, now, Vox's invasion of me had been a startling distraction. But I dared not let myself forget that we were in the midst of a traversal of heaven. The lives of us all, and of our passengers, depended on the proper execution of our duties: even mine. And worlds awaited the bounty that we bore. My task of the moment was to oversee spinaround acquisition.

I told Vox to leave me temporarily while I went through the routines of acquisition. I would be jacked to other crewmen for a time; they might very well be able to detect her within me; there was no telling what might happen. But she refused. "No," she said. "I won't leave you. I don't want to go out there. But I'll hide, deep down, the way I did when I was upset with you."

"Vox —" I began.

"No. Please. I don't want to talk about it."

There was no time to argue the point. I could feel the depth and intensity of her stubborn determination.

"Hide, then," I said. "If that's what you want to do."

I made my way down out of the Eye to Engine Deck.

The rest of the acquisition team was already assembled in the Great Navigation Hall: Fresco, Raebuck, Roacher. Raebuck's role was to see to it that communications channels were kept open, Fresco's to set up the navigation coordinates, and Roacher, as power engineer, would monitor fluctuations in drain and input-output cycling. My function was to give the cues at each stage of acquisition. In truth I was pretty much redundant, since Raebuck and Fresco and Roacher had been doing this sort of thing a dozen times a voyage for scores of voyages and they had little need of my guidance. The deeper truth was that they were redundant too, for 49 Henry Henry would oversee us all, and the intelligence was quite capable of setting up the entire process without any human help. Nevertheless there were formalities to observe, and not inane ones. Intelligences are far superior to humans in mental capacity, interfacing capability, and reaction time, but even so they are nothing but servants, and artificial servants at that, lacking in any real awareness of human fragility or human ethical complexity. They must only be used as tools, not decision-makers. A society which delegates responsibilities of life and death to its servants will eventually find the servants' hands at its throat. As for me, novice that I was, my role was valid as well: the focal point of the enterprise, the prime initiator, the conductor and observer of the process. Perhaps anyone could perform those functions, but the fact remained that *someone* had to, and by tradition that someone was the captain. Call it a ritual, call it a highly stylized dance, if you will. But there is no getting away from the human need for ritual and stylization. Such aspects of a process may not seem essential, but they are valuable and significant, and ultimately they can be seen to be essential as well.

"Shall we begin?" Fresco asked.

We jacked up, Roacher directly into the ship, Raebuck into Roacher, Fresco to me, me into the ship.

"Simulation," I said.

Raebuck keyed in the first code and the vast echoing space that was the Great Navigation Hall came alive with pulsing light: a representation of heaven all about us, the lines of force, the spinaround nodes, the stars, the planets. We moved unhinderedly in free fall, drifting as casually as angels. We could easily have believed we were starwalking.

The simulacrum of the ship was a bright arrow of fierce light just below us and to the left. Ahead, throbbing like a nest of twining angry serpents, was the globe that represented the Lasciate Ogni Speranza spinaround point, tightly-wound dull gray cables shot through with strands of fierce scarlet.

"Enter approach mode," I said. "Activate receptors. Begin threshold equalization. Begin momentum comparison. Prepare for acceleration uptick. Check angular velocity. Begin spin consolidation. Enter displacement select. Extend mast. Prepare for acquisition receptivity."

At each command the proper man touched a control key or pressed a directive panel or simply sent an impulse shooting through the jack hookup by which he was connected, directly or indirectly, to the mind of the ship. Out of courtesy to me, they waited until the commands were given, but the speed with which they obeyed told me that their minds were already in motion even as I spoke.

"It's really exciting, isn't it?" Vox said suddenly.

"For God's sake, Vox! What are you trying to do?"

For all I knew, the others had heard her outburst as clearly as though it had come across a loudspeaker.

"I mean," she went on, "I never imagined it was anything like this. I can feel the whole — "

I shot her a sharp, anguished order to keep quiet. Her surfacing like this, after my warning to her, was a lunatic act. In the silence that followed I felt a kind of inner reverberation, a sulky twanging of displeasure coming from her. But I had no time to worry about Vox's moods now.

Arcing patterns of displacement power went ricocheting through the Great Navigation Hall as our mast came forth — not the underpinning for a set of sails, as it would be on a vessel that plied planetary seas, but rather a giant antenna to link us to the spinaround point ahead — and the ship and the spinaround point reached toward one another like grappling many-armed wrestlers. Hot streaks of crimson and emerald and gold and amethyst speared the air, vaulting and rebounding. The spinaround point, activated now and trembling between energy states, was enfolding us in its million tentacles, capturing us, making ready to whirl on its axis and hurl us swiftly onward toward the next way-station in our journey across heaven.

"Acquisition," Raebuck announced.

"Proceed to capture acceptance," I said.

"Acceptance," said Raebuck.

"Directional mode," I said. "Dimensional grid eleven."

"Dimensional grid eleven," Fresco repeated.

The whole hall seemed on fire now.

"Wonderful," Vox murmured. "So beautiful—"

"Vox!"

"Request spin authorization," said Fresco.

"Spin authorization granted," I said. "Grid eleven."

"Grid eleven," Fresco said again. "Spin achieved."

A tremor went rippling through me—and through Fresco, through Raebuck, through Roacher. It was the ship, in the persona of 49 Henry Henry, completing the acquisition process. We had been captured by Lasciate Ogni Speranza, we had undergone velocity absorption and redirection, we had had new spin imparted to us, and we had been sent soaring off through heaven toward our upcoming port of call. I heard Vox sobbing within me, not a sob of despair but one of ecstasy, of fulfillment.

We all unjacked. Raebuck, that dour man, managed a little smile as he turned to me.

"Nicely done, captain," he said.

"Yes," said Fresco. "Very nice. You're a quick learner."

I saw Roacher studying me with those little shining eyes of his. Go on, you bastard, I thought. You give a compliment too now, if you know how.

But all he did was stare. I shrugged and turned away.

What Roacher thought or said made little difference to me, I told myself.

As we left the Great Navigation Hall in our separate directions Fresco fell in alongside me. Without a word we trudged together toward the transit trackers that were waiting for us. Just as I was about to board mine he — or was it she? — said softly, "Captain?"

"What is it, Fresco?"

Fresco leaned close. Soft sly eyes, tricksy little smile; and yet I felt some warmth coming from the navigator.

"It's a very dangerous game, captain."

"I don't know what you mean."

"Yes, you do," Fresco said. "No use pretending. We were jacked together in there. I felt things. I know."

There was nothing I could say, so I said nothing.

After a moment Fresco said, "I like you. I won't harm you. But Roacher knows too. I don't know if he knew before, but he certainly knows now. If I were you, I'd find that very troublesome, captain. Just a word to the wise. All right?"

ONLY A FOOL would have remained on such a course as I had been following. Vox saw the risks as well as I. There was no hiding anything from anyone any longer; if Roacher knew, then Bulgar knew, and soon it would be all over the ship. No question, either, but that 49 Henry Henry knew. In the intimacies of our navigation-hall contact, Vox must have been as apparent to them as a red scarf around my forehead.

There was no point in taking her to task for revealing her presence within me like that during acquisition. What was done was done. At first it had seemed impossible to understand why she had done such a thing; but then it became all too easy to comprehend. It was the same sort of unpredictable, unexamined, impulsive behavior that had led her to go barging into a suspended passenger's mind and cause his death. She was simply not one who paused to think before acting. That kind of behavior has always been bewildering to me. She was my opposite as well as my double. And yet had I not done a Vox-like thing myself, taking her into me, when she appealed to me for sanctuary, without stopping at all to consider the consequences?

"Where can I go?" she asked, desperate. "If I move around the ship freely again they'll track me and close me off. And then they'll eradicate me. They'll—"

"Easy," I said. "Don't panic. I'll hide you where they won't find you."

"Inside some passenger?"

"We can't try that again. There's no way to prepare the passenger for what's happening to him, and he'll panic. No. I'll put you in one of the annexes. Or maybe one of the virtualities."

"The what?"

"The additional cargo area. The subspace extensions that surround the ship."

She gasped. "Those aren't even real! I was in them, when I was traveling around the ship. Those are just clusters of probability waves!"

"You'll be safe there," I said.

"I'm afraid. It's bad enough that *I'm* not real any more. But to be stored in a place that isn't real either—"

"You're as real as I am. And the outstructures are just as real as the rest of the ship. It's a different quality of reality, that's all. Nothing bad will happen to you out there. You've told me yourself that you've already been in them, right? And got out again without any problems. They won't be able to detect you there, Vox. But I tell you this, that if you stay in me, or anywhere else in the main part of the ship, they'll track you down and find you and eradicate you. And probably eradicate me right along with you."

91

"Do you mean that?" she said, sounding chastened.

"Come on. There isn't much time."

On the pretext of a routine inventory check—well within my table of responsibilities—I obtained access to one of the virtualities. It was the storehouse where the probability stabilizers were kept. No one was likely to search for her there. The chances of our encountering a zone of probability turbulence between here and Cul-de-Sac were minimal; and in the ordinary course of a voyage nobody cared to enter any of the virtualities.

I had lied to Vox, or at least committed a half-truth, by leading her to believe that all our outstructures are of an equal level of reality. Certainly the annexes are tangible, solid; they differ from the ship proper only in the spin of their dimensional polarity. They are invisible except when activated, and they involve us in no additional expenditure of fuel, but there is no uncertainty about their existence, which is why we entrust valuable cargo to them, and on some occasions even passengers.

The extensions are a level further removed from basic reality. They are skewed not only in dimensional polarity but in temporal contiguity: that is, we carry them with us under time displacement, generally ten to twenty virtual years in the past or future. The risks of this are extremely minor and the payoff in reduction of generating cost is great. Still, we are measurably more cautious about what sort of cargo we keep in them.

As for the virtualities—

Their name itself implies their uncertainty. They are purely probabilistic entities, existing most of the time in the stochastic void that surrounds the ship. In

92

simpler words, whether they are actually there or not, at any given time is a matter worth wagering on. We know how to access them at the time of greatest probability, and our techniques are quite reliable, which is why we can use them for overflow ladings when our cargo uptake is unusually heavy. But in general we prefer not to entrust anything very important to them, since a virtuality's range of access times can fluctuate in an extreme way, from a matter of microseconds to a matter of megayears, and that can make quick recall a chancy affair.

Knowing all this, I put Vox in a virtuality anyway.

I had to hide her. And I had to hide her in a place where no one would look. The risk that I'd be unable to call her up again because of virtuality fluctuation was a small one. The risk was much greater that she would be detected, and she and I both punished, if I let her remain in any area of the ship that had a higher order of probability.

"I want you to stay here until the coast is clear," I told her sternly. "No impulsive journeys around the ship, no excursions into adjoining outstructures, no little trips of any kind, regardless of how restless you get. Is that clear? I'll call you up from here as soon as I think it's safe."

"I'll miss you, Adam."

"The same here. But this is how it has to be."

"I know."

"If you're discovered, I'll deny I know anything about you. I mean that, Vox."

"I understand."

"You won't be stuck in here long. I promise you that."

"Will you visit me?"

"That wouldn't be wise," I said.

"But maybe you will anyway."

"Maybe. I don't know." I opened the access channel. The virtuality gaped before us. "Go on," I said. "In with you. In. Now. Go, Vox. Go."

I could feel her leaving me. It was almost like an amputation. The silence, the emptiness, that descended on me suddenly was ten times as deep as what I had felt when she had merely been hiding within me. She was gone, now. For the first time in days, I was truly alone.

I closed off the virtuality.

When I returned to the Eye, Roacher was waiting for me near the command bridge.

"You have a moment, captain?"

"What is it, Roacher?"

"The missing matrix. We have proof it's still on board ship."

"Proof?"

"You know what I mean. You felt it just like I did while we were doing acquisition. It said something. It spoke. It was right in there in the navigation hall with us, captain."

I met his luminescent gaze levelly and said in an even voice, "I was giving my complete attention to what we were doing, Roacher. Spinaround acquisition isn't second nature to me the way it is to you. I had no time to notice any matrixes floating around in there."

"You didn't?"

"No. Does that disappoint you?"

"That might mean that you're the one carrying the matrix," he said.

"How so?"

"If it's in you, down on a subneural level, you might not even be aware of it. But we would be. Raebuck, Fresco, me. We all detected something, captain. If it wasn't in us it would have to be in you. We can't have a matrix riding around inside our captain, you know. No telling how that could distort his judgment. What dangers that might lead us into."

"I'm not carrying any matrixes, Roacher."

"Can we be sure of that?"

"Would you like to have a look?"

"A jackup, you mean? You and me?"

The notion disgusted me. But I had to make the offer.

"A — jackup, yes," I said. "Communion. You and me, Roacher. Right now. Come on, we'll measure the bandwidths and do the matching. Let's get this over with."

He contemplated me a long while, as if calculating the likelihood that I was bluffing. In the end he must have decided that I was too naive to be able to play the game out to so hazardous a turn. He knew that I wouldn't bluff, that I was confident he would find me untenanted or I never would have made the offer.

"No," he said finally. "We don't need to bother with that."

"Are you sure?"

"If you say you're clean — "

"But I might be carrying her and not even know it," I said. "You told me that yourself."

"Forget it. You'd know, if you had her in you."

"You'll never be certain of that unless you look. Let's jack up, Roacher."

He scowled. "Forget it," he said again, and turned away. "You must be clean, if you're this eager for jacking. But I'll tell you this, captain. We're going to find her, wherever she's hiding. And when we do — "

He left the threat unfinished. I stood staring at his retreating form until he was lost to view.

FOR A FEW DAYS everything seemed back to normal. We sped onward toward Cul-de-Sac. I went through the round of my regular tasks, however meaningless they seemed to me. Most of them did. I had not yet achieved any sense that the *Sword of Orion* was under my command in anything but the most hypothetical way. Still, I did what I had to do.

No one spoke of the missing matrix within my hearing. On those rare occasions when I encountered some other member of the crew while I moved about the ship, I could tell by the hooded look of his eyes that I was still under suspicion. But they had no proof. The matrix was no longer in any way evident on board. The ship's intelligences were unable to find the slightest trace of its presence.

I was alone, and oh! it was a painful business for me.

I suppose that once you have tasted that kind of round-the-clock communion, that sort of perpetual jacking, you are never the same again. I don't know: there is no real information available on cases of possession by free matrix, only shipboard folklore, scarcely to be taken seriously. All I can judge by is my own misery now that Vox was actually gone. She was only a half-grown girl, a wild coltish thing, unstable, unformed; and yet, she had lived within me and we had come toward one another to construct the deepest sort of sharing, what was almost a kind of marriage. You could call it that.

After five or six days I knew I had to see her again. Whatever the risks.

I accessed the virtuality and sent a signal into it that I was coming in. There was no reply; and for one terrible moment I feared the worst, that in the mysterious workings of the virtuality she had somehow been engulfed and destroyed. But that was not the case. I stepped through the glowing pink-edged field of light that was the gateway to the virtuality, and instantly I felt her near me, clinging tight, trembling with joy.

She held back, though, from entering me. She wanted me to tell her it was safe. I beckoned her in; and then came that sharp warm sensation I remembered so well, as she slipped down into my neural network and we became one.

"I can only stay a little while," I said. "It's still very chancy for me to be with you."

"Oh, Adam, Adam, it's been so awful for me in here—"

"I know. I can imagine."

"Are they still looking for me?"

"I think they're starting to put you out of their minds," I said. And we both laughed at the play on words that the phrase implied.

I didn't dare remain more than a few minutes. I had only wanted to touch souls with her briefly, to reassure myself that she was all right and to ease the pain of separation. But it was irregular for a captain to enter a virtuality at all. To stay in one for any length of time exposed me to real risk of detection.

But my next visit was longer, and the one after that longer still. We were like furtive lovers meeting in a dark forest for hasty delicious trysts. Hidden there in that not-quite-real outstructure of the ship we would join our two selves and whisper together with urgent intensity until I felt it was time for me to leave. She would always try to keep me longer; but her resistance to my departure was never great, nor did she ever suggest accompanying me back into the stable sector of the ship. She had come to understand that the only place we could meet was in the virtuality.

We were nearing the vicinity of Cul-de-Sac now. Soon we would go to worldward and the shoreships would travel out to meet us, so that we could download the cargo that was meant for them. It was time to begin considering the problem of what would happen to Vox when we reached our destination.

That was something I was unwilling to face. However I tried, I could not force myself to confront the difficulties that I knew lay just ahead.

But she could.

"We must be getting close to Cul-de-Sac now," she said.

"We'll be there soon, yes."

"I've been thinking about that. How I'm going to deal with that."

"What do you mean?"

"I'm a lost soul," she said. "Literally. There's no way I can come to life again."

"I don't under—"

"Adam, don't you see?" she cried fiercely. "I can't just float down to Cul-de-Sac and grab myself a body and put myself on the roster of colonists. And you can't possibly smuggle me down there while nobody's looking. The first time anyone ran an inventory check, or did passport control, I'd be dead. No, the only way I can get there is to be neatly packed up again in my original storage circuit. And even if I could figure out how to get back into that, I'd be simply handing myself over for punishment or even eradication. I'm listed as missing on the manifest, right? And I'm wanted for causing the death of that passenger. Now I turn up again, in my storage circuit. You think they'll just download me nicely to Cul-de-Sac and give me the body that's waiting for me there? Not very likely. Not likely that I'll ever get out of that circuit alive, is it, once I go back in? Assuming I *could* go back in in the first place. I don't know how a storage circuit is operated, do you? And there's nobody you can ask."

"What are you trying to say, Vox?"

"I'm not trying to say anything. I'm saying it. I have to leave the ship on my own and disappear."

"No. You can't do that!"

"Sure I can. It'll be just like starwalking. I can go anywhere I please. Right through the skin of the ship, out into heaven. And keep on going."

"To Cul-de-Sac?"

"You're being stupid," she said. "Not to Cul-de-Sac, no. Not to anywhere. That's all over for me, the idea of getting a new body. I have no legal existence any more. I've messed myself up. All right: I admit it. I'll take what's coming to me. It won't be so bad, Adam. I'll go starwalking. Outward and outward and outward, forever and ever."

"You mustn't," I said. "Stay here with me."

"Where? In this empty storage unit out here?"

"No," I told her. "Within me. The way we are right now. The way we were before."

"How long do you think we could carry that off?" she asked.

I didn't answer.

"Every time you have to jack into the machinery I'll have to hide myself down deep," she said. "And I can't guarantee that I'll go deep enough, or that I'll stay down there long enough. Sooner or later they'll notice me. They'll find me. They'll eradicate me and they'll throw you out of the Service, or maybe they'll eradicate you too. No, Adam. It couldn't possibly work. And I'm not going to destroy you with me. I've done enough harm to you already."

"Vox —"

"No. This is how it has to be."

AND THIS IS HOW IT WAS. We were deep in the Spook Cluster now, and the Vainglory Archipelago burned bright on my realspace screen. Somewhere down there was the planet called Cul-de-Sac. Before we came to worldward of it, Vox would have to slip away into the great night of heaven.

Making a worldward approach is perhaps the most difficult maneuver a starship must achieve; and the captain must go to the edge of his abilities along with everyone else. Novice at my trade though I was, I would be called on to perform complex and challenging processes. If I failed at them, other crewmen might cut in and intervene, or, if necessary, the ship's intelligences might override; but if that came to pass my career would be destroyed, and there was the small but finite possibility, I suppose, that the ship itself could be gravely damaged or even lost.

I was determined, all the same, to give Vox the best send-off I could.

On the morning of our approach I stood for a time on

Outerscreen Level, staring down at the world that called itself Cul-de-Sac. It glowed like a red eye in the night. I knew that it was the world Vox had chosen for herself, but all the same it seemed repellent to me, almost evil. I felt that way about all the worlds of the shore people now. The Service had changed me; and I knew that the change was irreversible. Never again would I go down to one of those worlds. The starship was my world now.

I went to the virtuality where Vox was waiting.

"Come," I said, and she entered me.

Together we crossed the ship to the Great Navigation Hall.

The approach team had already gathered: Raebuck, Fresco, Roacher, again, along with Pedregal, who would supervise the downloading of cargo. The intelligence on duty was 612 Jason. I greeted them with quick nods and we jacked ourselves together in approach series.

Almost at once I felt Roacher probing within me, searching for the fugitive intelligence that he still thought I might be harboring. Vox shrank back, deep out of sight. I didn't care. Let him probe, I thought. This will all be over soon.

"Request approach instructions," Fresco said.

"Simulation," I ordered.

The fiery red eye of Cul-de-Sac sprang into vivid representation before us in the hall. On the other side of us was the simulacrum of the ship, surrounded by sheets of white flame that rippled like the blaze of the aurora.

I gave the command and we entered approach mode.

We could not, of course, come closer to planetskin

than a million shiplengths, or Cul-de-Sac's inexorable forces would rip us apart. But we had to line the ship up with its extended mast aimed at the planet's equator, and hold ourselves firm in that position while the shoreships of Cul-de-Sac came swarming up from their red world to receive their cargo from us.

612 Jason fed me the coordinates and I gave them to Fresco, while Raebuck kept the channels clear and Roacher saw to it that we had enough power for what we had to do. But as I passed the data along to Fresco, it was with every sign reversed. My purpose was to aim the mast not downward to Cul-de-Sac but outward toward the stars of heaven.

At first none of them noticed. Everything seemed to be going serenely. Because my reversals were exact, only the closest examination of the ship's position would indicate our 180-degree displacement.

Floating in the free fall of the Great Navigation Hall, I felt almost as though I could detect the movements of the ship. An illusion, I knew. But a powerful one. The vast ten-kilometer-long needle that was the *Sword of Orion* seemed to hang suspended, motionless, and then to begin slowly, slowly to turn, tipping itself on its axis, reaching for the stars with its mighty mast. Easily, easily, slowly, silently —

What joy that was, feeling the ship in my hand!

The ship was mine. I had mastered it.

"Captain," Fresco said softly.

"Easy on, Fresco. Keep feeding power."

"Captain, the signs don't look right — "

"Easy on. Easy."

"Give me a coordinates check, captain."

"Another minute," I told him.

"But — "

"Easy on, Fresco."

Now I felt restlessness too from Pedregal, and a slow chilly stirring of interrogation from Raebuck; and then Roacher probed me again, perhaps seeking Vox, perhaps simply trying to discover what was going on. They knew something was wrong, but they weren't sure what it was.

We were nearly at full extension, now. Within me there was an electrical trembling: Vox rising through the levels of my mind, nearing the surface, preparing for departure.

"Captain, we're turned the wrong way!" Fresco cried.

"I know," I said. "Easy on. We'll swing around in a moment."

"He's gone crazy!" Pedregal blurted.

I felt Vox slipping free of my mind. But somehow I found myself still aware of her movements, I suppose because I was jacked into 612 Jason and 612 Jason was monitoring everything. Easily, serenely, Vox melted into the skin of the ship.

"*Captain!*" Fresco yelled, and began to struggle with me for control.

I held the navigator at arm's length and watched in a strange and wonderful calmness as Vox passed through the ship's circuitry all in an instant and emerged at the tip of the mast, facing the stars. And cast herself adrift.

Because I had turned the ship around, she could not be captured and acquired by Cul-de-Sac's powerful navigational grid, but would be free to move outward into heaven. For her it would be a kind of floating out to sea, now. After a time she would be so far out that she could no longer key into the shipboard bioprocessors that sustained the patterns of her consciousness, and, though the web of electrical impulses that was the Vox matrix would travel outward and onward forever, the set of identity responses that was Vox herself would lose focus soon, would begin to waver and blur. In a little while, or perhaps not so little, but inevitably, her sense of herself as an independent entity would be lost. Which is to say, she would die.

I followed her as long as I could. I saw a spark traveling across the great night. And then nothing.

"All right," I said to Fresco. "Now let's turn the ship the right way around and give them their cargo."

THAT WAS MANY YEARS AGO. Perhaps no one else remembers those events, which seem so dreamlike now even to me. The *Sword of Orion* has carried me nearly everywhere in the galaxy since then. On some voyages I have been captain; on others, a downloader, a supercargo, a mind-wiper, even sometimes a push-cell. It makes no difference how we serve, in the Service.

I often think of her. There was a time when thinking of her meant coming to terms with feelings of grief and pain and irrecoverable loss, but no longer, not for many years. She must be long dead now, however durable and resilient the spark of her might have been. And yet she still lives. Of that much I am certain. There is a place within me where I can reach her warmth, her strength, her quirky vitality, her impulsive suddenness. I can feel those aspects of her, those gifts of her brief time of sanctuary within me, as a living presence still, and I think I always will, as I make my way from world to tethered world, as I journey onward everlastingly spanning the dark light-years in this great ship of heaven.